Heart of Steele

Adelle Laudan

Heart of Steele

by

Adelle Laudan

2nd Edition

Cover Art by Adelle Laudan

ISBN: 978-1-927700-03-7
ASIN: B00HHIN0AK

.

Previously published by Passion In Print Publishing

Heart of Steele – 2nd Edition

Fully revised.

Adelle Laudan

http://adellelaudan.com

Dedicated
to

~Jeff~

~Cam~

~Victoria~

~Nate~

Four awesome young adults who
keep me young with their hilarious antics.
Thanks for always remembering
I take two creams, no sugar.

Chapter One

It seems right now that all I've done in my life is make my way here to you.

Kara pressed the book to her breasts and sighed. In her mind's eye, she pictured the ruggedly handsome Clint Eastwood playing the part of Robert Kincaid in the film version of *The Bridges of Madison County*.

If only men talked like this in real life.

Her gaze travelled over row upon row of bookcases filled to capacity. How she loved spending her lunch hours in this bookstore.

"So what did you think of the passage I marked out for you?" Abe shuffled past boxes of unopened books with two cups of tea in his weathered hands. "Robert Waller sure has a way with words, don't you think?"

Kara smiled. "I've heard so many different things about his writing. But you can't dispute he has the gift of taking everyday issues and making them intimate in the simplest of ways."

Abe set the cups down on a small card table wedged between their chairs. "I thought you'd like it."

She closed the book, returned it to the shelf beside her, and sipped from her tea. "Mmm, I love honey in my tea."

"I think you're sweet enough without it."

Heat rushed to her cheeks. Abe's handsome grandson, Noah,

filled the doorway; his mouth turned up in a devilish grin.

"You're a smooth talker, Noah." Abe cleared a stack of books off of the chair beside his. "You're just in time for tea."

"What, no desserts today?" He pouted.

Kara smiled and retrieved a pastry box from under her chair. "You didn't actually think I'd come empty handed, did you?"

Noah's grandfather stood between him and the box. "You keep your big mitts out of there until I get back with your tea." He scolded while shaking a finger in his face.

Noah put up his hands in surrender. "Yes, sir!"

Kara's heartbeat quickened as it always did when left alone with Noah. Lately he'd taken to dropping in more often during her lunch dates with Abe.

"What have you been reading today?" He leaned back in his chair, the thin fabric of his t-shirt pulled taut across his broad chest.

Her fingers itched to free his honey-blond hair from the confines of his ever-present pony tail. Unfortunately, every time he showed up, her mind turned to mush. "Um..." Unable to remember the author's name, she pulled the book from the shelf.

Noah took the hardback from her. His fingers touched hers, sending a tingly sensation up her arm—her breath hitched.

"Robert James Waller. Have you read any of his other work? *A Thousand Country Roads* is a good one."

Kara shook her head, surprised he'd be so knowledgeable about such a romantic writer.

"Here you go." Abe handed his grandson a steaming mug and returned to his seat.

"Thanks, Gramps."

Abe rubbed his hands together. He raised his bushy white brows in anticipation as she opened the box. "Oh dear, you've really outdone yourself this time Kara."

She shrugged. "It's just cheesecake." From a bag hanging from her chair, she produced three small plates and plastic forks. "You're my guinea pigs today. It's a new recipe, Sugar Shack Maple Walnut Cheesecake. Made with genuine Ontario maple syrup."

"How could anything with a name like that taste bad?" Noah used one finger to catch the maple syrup that dripped down the side of the box and licked it. "Mmm..."

Flustered, Kara coughed and turned her head, glancing at her watch. "Oh, my. Would you look at the time?" She fumbled with her purse, purposely avoiding Noah's stare. She kissed Abe's cheek. "I've got to run. We've got a big order for a shindig over at Steele Towers tomorrow night. Ada and Fred are pretty excited about it. It could mean regular business and a huge hike in profits for the bakery."

She watched Abe and his grandson exchange an odd look. She couldn't help but wonder what it meant.

"Impressive." Abe took a square from the box without looking up at her. "Thanks for the cheesecake."

Kara's frowned. "Try to control your enthusiasm boys." She slung her purse over her shoulder. "You might want to save some of that for tomorrow. I doubt I'll be able to get away."

The two men grunted with mouths full of cheesecake.

Kara left the bookstore shaking her head. "Men!"

Joni curled up on the couch beside her, and Kara worked her fingers through her daughter's unruly mass of auburn curls. For as far back as she could remember, Joni loved it when someone played with her hair.

"How was school today?"

"Same as always. I can't wait to go to college." She yawned. "It seems like only yesterday you were changing my diapers." She mimicked her mother. A smile played at the corners of her mouth.

Kara pulled the pillow out from behind her and smacked her on the head. "Ha, ha, very funny."

"Hey!" Joni yanked the pillow away and bolted from the sofa. "Isn't it past your bedtime?"

A yawn threatened to escape, and Kara coughed in her hand. "Actually, I better get to bed soon. We have a big order to fill tomorrow."

"Nice! Is it a new customer?" Her daughter plunked down in an overstuffed armchair across from her.

"Steele Towers."

Joni's eyebrows arched. "The same Steele...?"

Kara shrugged. "Steele Enterprises is a huge corporation. I doubt the hotel has anything to do with the financial end of things."

"How do you feel about doing business with them? After all, if it wasn't for Steele Enterprises, we'd still be living in our house."

Kara sighed. "Well, I guess their money is as good as the next multi-million dollar corporations." She picked up her water glass from the coffee table and stood. "Besides, it's a great opportunity for the bakery. I can't very well ask Fred and Ada not to take the order because your father owed them money and we were forced to sell the house after he passed to settle his debt."

Joni jumped up and wrapped her arms around her. "You're right. Besides, I kind of like living in the city now that we're here."

Kara gave her a final squeeze. "The bottom line is men are trouble." She snickered. "We'll be just fine on our own."

"You betcha." Joni took the glass from her hand. "You go on up to bed, I'll set your coffee for the morning."

Kara kissed her forehead. "Works for me." She stifled a yawn. "I love you, Joni."

"What's not to love?" She sauntered away, flicking her hair over her shoulder.

Chapter Two

Kara struggled with the relic steering wheel of a delivery truck that should have made its way to the scrap yard years ago. Her body, already sore and tired from a long day of making desserts, screamed in defiance as she weaved her way in and around Steele Towers' filled-to-capacity parking lot.

She'd never seen her bosses so fired up about an order. So, when Fred unexpectedly went home sick and Ada had asked her to make the delivery, she could hardly say no. They'd treated her and Joni like family for almost five years now.

The truck's headlights illuminated the loading dock where a handsome young man in an expensive-looking suit paced back and forth. He checked his watch and ran his fingers back through a head of thick, blond hair.

She backed up to the delivery doors and jumped down from the driver's side in time to see him shake his head and check his watch yet again.

His good looks dissipated the moment he opened his mouth. "Well, it's about time." He glared at her and tapped the watch.

"I'm sorry. I know we're cutting it close, but I promise our desserts will more than make up for the delay."

His looked her up and down, his disgust almost palpable. "Well, come on. Bring your goods to the kitchen immediately." He looked past her, his brow creasing. "I do hope your servers are dressed more appropriately."

"Servers? I'm afraid there's been a misunderstanding. Whoever placed the order, assured us there would be staff available to help unload."

"Miss..."

"Walker, Kara Walker."

"Caleb Steele. This is a rather unfortunate situation." He shook his head. "Open the back. We'll have to unload ourselves." He folded his arms across his chest and watched her fight with the heavy latch before opening the door, tapping his foot impatiently. "Time is of the essence."

Who the hell does he think he is? If this order wasn't so important to the bakery she'd have a few choice words for Caleb Steele. Lucky for him, he kept his mouth shut and helped her unload the desserts. Once they had delivered the last tray to the kitchen, she returned and closed the truck door, anxious to put some distance between them.

"You can leave it parked here."

Her brow arched questioningly. "Pardon me?"

"Surely you don't think you're going to leave me to serve the desserts myself? I insist on your help."

Her laughter bubbled up and spilled out. "In case you haven't noticed, I'm hardly dressed to play hostess to a room full of doctors."

"Of course I noticed." His hands flew to his slender hips. "This is no time to worry about looking pretty. There's a job to be done."

Anger flashed up within her. "How dare you!"

Caleb Steele held up his hands in defence. "Now, now, there's no time for drama. I'll go try and find some help. Be sure the trays are uncovered and ready by the time I get back."

He left before she had a chance to reply. Never had a customer made her so angry. She'd definitely be placing a call to his boss once this god-awful night was behind her. Kara carefully removed all of the lids from the trays, relieved they had all made it intact. At least Mr. Hoity Toity wouldn't be able to say anything about the quality of her desserts.

Kara stacked the lids at the end of the counter. She'd just finished putting her hair up in a twist when Caleb Steele burst through the door with two rather frazzled employees in tow. They filed in and stood next to her while she attempted to tame a couple of fiery ringlets that had escaped the confines of the twist.

The tight-lipped trio remained silent.

"Good. Try not to drop anything. I'm sure we're being charged a small fortune for these confections."

Kara shot daggers at him for his smart-ass comment. She set down her first tray and purposely ignored Caleb, who stood at the edge of the hall, watching their every move. *If he thinks the desserts are expensive, wait until he gets my bill for serving them.*

For the most part, the tables of doctors were engrossed in conversations she couldn't even begin to decipher. She returned the occasional smile and otherwise carried on with the task at hand. By the time they finished the rounds, her poor feet throbbed. She'd walked her ass off earlier getting the order ready on top of her other daily duties. The only good thing about being coerced into playing waitress was the many compliments she'd overheard about her delicacies. At the end of dessert, there wasn't even one square left on any of the nine platters. No leftovers—it didn't get much better than that. Now, if she could escape without any further conversation with Mr. Steele, which would be the perfect end to her day. She winced when she realized that wouldn't be the case.

Caleb held the kitchen doors open for Kara and the other two servers. "Thank you all for filling in and getting the job done. I don't think anyone even noticed your lack of experience." His gaze flitted from one to the other.

The jerk can't even give a proper thank you. "If that's all, I really need to be getting the truck back to the shop," Kara piped in, anxious to leave.

Caleb nodded curtly. "Yes, Ms. Walker, I'll be sure to put in a good word with your employer first chance I get."

Kara feigned a smile. *You be sure to do that*. She stifled the urge to laugh. *I'm sure Ada and Fred will have a few things to say to you as well.*

The kitchen doors swung open, and her eyes widened in surprise. Abe's grandson strolled in. What were the odds of running into him here?

The corners of his mouth lifted in a devilish smile—the perfect complement to the mischievous glint in his brown eyes. "Am I too late? I hope you saved me some dessert, dear brother."

Brother? Why didn't he say anything after I told him about the big order Steele Towers had placed?

He slapped his somewhat stunned brother on the back. The two men looked nothing alike. Caleb Steele dressed immaculately in a well-tailored suit and tie. Not one blond curl out of place. His brother, Noah, stood at least six inches taller, wearing worn, fitted jeans and a black button-down shirt. His honey blond hair bone straight and tied back in a pony tail.

"Where have you been?" Caleb sounded more like a father than a sibling. "Do you realize you almost ruined the dinner I've been painstakingly organizing for over a month?"

Seemingly amused, Noah infuriated Caleb by patting the top of his head. "Now, now, little bro, I'm sure it wasn't as bad as you make it out to be."

Noah sauntered over to her. The masculine scent of musk filled her senses and sent her pulse racing.

"And why, pray tell is the genius behind these delicacies serving them to a bunch of uptight doctors?"

"What are you talking about?" replied Caleb. "This is Kara Walker, the delivery girl from the bakery."

Noah tilted back his head and laughed. "Do you want to tell him, or can I?"

Kara shrugged, feigning indifference. Despite her confusion as to why Noah was there to begin with, she enjoyed watching his pompous-ass brother squirm. "I figured he'd find out on his own." She stared intently into Caleb's bewildered eyes. "I'd love to stick around and chat some more, but I've been on my feet since early this morning. Mr. Steele, you can expect a bill for the desserts—with the addition of my services for this evening." She turned on her heel and moved toward the door. She looked back over her shoulder. "And I can assure you, I don't come cheap."

Noah's laughter followed her out the door to the truck. She guided the mechanical beast out of the parking lot and slammed on the brakes. Her jaw dropped. The bright neon sign of the hotel flashed...*Steele Towers.* "Shit!" Kara smacked the steering wheel. Pieces of the puzzle fell into place.

Steele...that means Abe is a Steele as well. Why would a man with all that money run a bookstore? If Noah placed the order for the hotel like Caleb said he did, then why didn't he say anything to me about it? None of this makes any sense.

What the hell is going on?

Chapter Three

Caleb and him were like oil and water much of the time, but he couldn't remember ever being so pissed at him. "I can't believe you had her waiting on tables."

His brother sat behind his pristine desk, looking very full of himself. "How was I to know who she was? She certainly didn't offer the information. If you had told me about the arrangements to begin with, none of this would have happened."

Noah clenched his hands so tightly his knuckles turned white. "Well, thanks to you, we'll be lucky if we can ever get them to fill another order for us."

Caleb shrugged matter-of-factly. "You know how I feel about hiring outside help."

Noah threw up his hands in exasperation. "I can't wait until Father gets back from his trip abroad. Do you have any idea how many staff members we've lost since he left you in charge?"

The veins on Caleb's neck bulged as they always did when he lost his temper. Zachary Steele had actually left them both in charge in his absence, but Caleb readily took command. He jumped at any opportunity to prove to his father he had what it took to be his successor one day. Noah gladly kept in the background. Occasionally he intervened when power swelled his little brother's head a tad too big for his own good.

"You win! You can take care of the whole show, but don't come crying to me when the crew jumps ship."

"Why don't you go talk romance novels with our dear grandfather in that old, dilapidated book store of his? God only knows what you find so fascinating about him."

"I might do just that. While I'm in the neighbourhood, I'll pay Ms. Walker a visit. Hopefully, I can convince her to accept my apology for your behaviour."

Noah stormed out of the office before he said or did

something he might regret later. He prayed Kara Walker would let him make amends. She certainly looked surprised to see him, undoubtedly a tad confused as to why he never mentioned he was a Steele, especially after she'd told them about the big order. There'd been several occasions when he'd almost came out with it, told her the truth about himself, but he didn't want to take the chance she'd be like so many other women from his past—dollar signs flashing in their eyes the moment they heard he was a Steele. Kara didn't seem like the type to be very impressed with his station in life, but he couldn't chance it. He didn't ever remember being so attracted to a woman as he was to her.

Kara slept through the alarm. It had taken her a long time to wind down from the events of last evening. Besides the fact that her time with Caleb had been an utter nightmare, she'd learned the real identity of Abe and his grandson. She tried to recall the first time she'd met Abe. Why didn't he reveal his last name then? How is it she'd never asked before now?

She couldn't help but wonder if Noah knew how she'd been forced to sell the farmhouse to pay off her late husband's debt. How many good laughs had they shared at her expense? To think Noah almost convinced her that not all men were underhanded bullies. *Sucker*. She prayed Abe was just an innocent bystander.

Thankfully, the gods were on her side, and the dreaded bus trip to work was quieter than usual. She broke her routine of getting off a couple stops early and rode directly to work, rather than chance a run-in with Noah Steele.

Ada stood at the bus stop waiting for her to arrive. "Oh Kara, I'm so sorry. I never would have asked you to make the delivery if I'd known they'd put you to work."

"Don't worry. How were you to know?"

Ada ushered her inside and led her to an oversized chair in the office. "Now you just sit there and relax while I pour us both a nice hot cup of coffee."

"That's really not necessary." She made a move to stand, but her overwrought friend held her shoulder to prevent her from standing.

"Indulge an old lady. I want to hear exactly what happened last night."

Kara sat back and replayed her time at Steele Towers.

Ada's eyes grew big and her jaw dropped as she listened. "Why on earth didn't you tell them you're our baker?"

Kara shrugged. "It all happened so fast. I actually had to stop myself from throttling the pompous jerk on a couple occasions. " She'd been pissed off at Noah for keeping his identity from her, yet she was guilty of the doing the same to Caleb. "Besides, it's not like I'm a celebrity or something like that. The desserts needed to be served."

"Well, I can assure you you'll never have to deal with any of them again. We won't be doing business with Steele Towers again."

"Now Ada, I understand your anger. Trust me; it's been a very long time since I've been so royally pissed off. Steele Towers can be very good for business."

"I don't know...."

Kara stood and put a hand on her friend's shoulder. "I think we just need to calm down before making any rash decisions, okay?"

"I'll try, but if Caleb Steele calls, I can't make any promises I won't give him a piece of my mind."

Laughter spilled out of Kara. She hoped to be half as feisty as Ada when she reached her seventies. "Let's just go about business as normal. The last thing I want to deal with today is anyone or anything related to the Steele family."

Ada linked an arm through hers and joined in her amusement as they left the office. Fred tried to bring up the subject on a couple of occasions during the course of the day, but she stopped him in mid-sentence. Luckily the bakery was busier than normal, leaving none of them with much time for anything. Replenishing the front showcase had been a job in itself.

"Phew." Ada mopped her sweaty face with the hem of her apron. "I'd say you impressed more than one doctor last night."

Kara cocked her head. "What?"

"I bet every one of their wives have been in today to check out the dessert their husband's raved about last night."

"You're kidding, right?"

Ada fanned the bundle of orders in her hand. "Nope. We have orders for birthdays, luncheons, and more." She waved the stack in Kara's face. "And this is only a few of them."

The bell above the shop door announced the arrival of a fresh group of customers. Kara hardly had time to stop and catch her breath, never mind trying to sort out the twister of emotions in her head. She was grateful for the increase in business, but she couldn't shake the feeling she'd been duped by both Noah and Abe. She'd never been so happy to flip the sign in the window to CLOSED, despite the fact she was no closer to a resolution in her mind.

Chapter Four

Noah spent every lunch hour at the bookstore in hopes of running into Kara Walker again. She hadn't so much as glanced through the window since the incident at Steele Towers. He didn't blame her for being pissed off. Knowing his brother, he probably put her through the wringer with his holier-than-thou attitude.

"Why don't you just walk up the street and talk to the woman?" Abe stepped down from the rolling ladder that allowed him access to the top book shelves.

"You're a mind reader now?" Noah chuckled at the old man who'd been more a dad to him than his own father had been.

"Let's just say I didn't get this old without learning a thing or two."

Noah sighed wearily. "I don't think I'm on her list of people she wants to see again."

"I've never seen you so fired up over a woman. Are you just going to let your brother screw that up for you?"

"If it was as simple as that, I'd have already been there." He stretched his long legs out in front of him. "So tell me something...."

"Shoot." Abe Steele sat across the table from his grandson.

"Why didn't you ever tell Kara who you are? More importantly, why didn't I?"

Abe shrugged. "I don't make a habit of it. I've never been much into the whole Steele-Empire label. I'm quite happy where I am."

"That's partly true for me. I guess I never filled the role my father would have liked. I figured Caleb seemed to thrive on it, so he's welcome to it."

"Maybe I never should have suggested the hotel place an order with the bakery. That woman sure is an artist when it comes to the desserts she makes; it seems such a shame not to share it."

"Well," said Noah, "I'm the one who jumped all over it and stepped on little brother's toes."

"I guess we're both a couple of chumps." Abe winked.

Noah laughed at the comical expression on his face. Maybe if they both extended their apologies to Kara, she'd forgive them? How could anyone resist the antics of Abe Steele?

"Well if she isn't going to bring me any more treats, I guess I'll just have to go get some myself."

"You're doing it again."

"What?" Abe waved away the comment and stood. "I have no idea what you're talking about."

"Want me to come along?"

"Nah, I think I can handle this one. Why don't you make yourself useful and chase some dust around this place?"

Noah welcomed the distraction. If he didn't keep busy, he'd go crazy waiting for Abe to come back.

"Stay off of the ladders. I don't want to come back and find you sprawled on the floor."

Abe ran his hand down the length of his dusty walking stick. On his way out of the store, he leaned heavily on the cane. If there was any chance of garnering Kara Walker's forgiveness, it would be his grandfather who could make it happen...and it looked like he was willing to go to any lengths to ensure his success.

Kara looked up from cutting pastry to see Abe step into the store. She couldn't hear what went on, but she could clearly see the store front. He perused the room, nodding his approval. Awkwardly, he walked with a cane to the front counter. Funny, she didn't remember him using one before. *Did he hurt himself climbing one of the ladders in the book store?*

Ada listened to Abe for a few moments before a smile filled her flushed face, and the two began to talk animatedly. She'd give anything to hear what they were saying. Ada held up a finger to Abe for him to wait, and Kara knew she was coming to get her. She wanted to go hide in the bathroom, but her legs betrayed her.

"What does he want?" Kara blurted out.

"Besides having withdrawals from not getting his weekly fill of desserts, he wants to talk to you." Ada shook her head. "I don't understand why you're being so rude. Did he do something to upset you?"

Kara slapped her rag on the counter. "Did he happen to mention his last name is Steele?"

Ada's jaw dropped.

"I didn't think so. All the lunch hours I spent with him and his grandson, and neither one felt the need to tell me? Not even after I told them about the big order?"

"Why don't you just talk to the man? At least find out why they didn't tell you."

Before she could protest, Ada was at her side, nudging her toward the door. Kara wiped her hands on her apron and shrugged her hands away. "Alright, I can walk on my own."

Abe beamed up at her as she walked in the room. "Kara, I've missed you." His voice filled with genuine sincerity. "Can you take a short break to indulge an old man?"

Kara wasn't sure if she wanted to hear anything he had to say, but she found herself following him out to the bench in front of the store. She watched the man she'd grown so close to over the past year lean heavily on his cane and lower himself to the bench. Despite how betrayed she felt, concern won over.

"Are you okay?"

He squeezed her knee. "Don't you worry; my arthritis always flares up after a good rain." He cleared his throat noisily. "I'm sorry things turned out the way they did the other night. I never would have suggested your delicacies for the hotel if I knew Caleb was going to be such an ass."

"*You* suggested?" His confession only managed to confuse her further.

"I had the best intentions. I guess that will teach me for sticking my nose in where it doesn't belong."

"Why wouldn't it belong? You're the founding Steele of Steele Enterprises aren't you?"

Abe sighed, looking very old all of a sudden. "My son has done very well for himself, but I'm afraid he deserves most of the credit for the business success."

"You mean to tell me you have nothing to do with it?" Kara watched for any tell-tale shifts in his demeanor that might expose his lies. She was very happy to find only the truth in his expressive eyes.

"I'm happy with my bookstore. I have no desire to be a part of the corporate world."

"Unlike your grandsons?" *Please tell me Noah feels the same way about his station in life*.

"I'm sure you've drawn a few of your own conclusions. Rest assured, Noah and I had no intention of hurting you. We'd both rather be judged by our own merits than by our affiliation with the Steele name."

She wanted to believe him. "It's not so much the Steele name, but why you both felt the need to keep it from me. You had to know it would come up sooner or later."

Abe sighed. "I guess you're right." He looked at her in all seriousness. "If you knew from the beginning I was a Steele would it have made a difference? Or for that matter, would you have opened yourself to our discussions about books with my grandson if you'd known?"

Kara weighed his words. She had to admit he'd made a valid point. Regardless, she couldn't shake the feeling they'd been dishonest, and she'd had enough dishonesty in her lifetime, not to mention the bad taste in her mouth from her first encounter with Steele Enterprises after her husband had died. "I don't know, Abe." She tried to gage the level of sincerity in his eyes. "Why didn't you tell me you were going to recommend me for the hotel?"

He shrugged. "I thought it would be a nice surprise, not to mention good for business."

She glanced at her watch. "I really should get back to work. We're swamped today."

"I hope your introduction to that group of doctors has

something to do with that."

The corners of her mouth lifted. "I guess I do have you to thank for that."

Abe smiled. "I hope you'll come and visit with me soon. I miss having someone to talk to who loves books as much as I do."

Kara nodded, resisting the urge to comment. She needed time to digest everything. "You take care of that leg."

Chapter Five

"I don't know why we didn't offer Joni a job here a long time ago." Ada placed an empty tray next to the sink. "The customers love her."

"Not to mention how much I enjoy having her here. Before long, she'll be off to college." Kara and Ada watched Joni round the counter to greet one of their regular customers. The elderly man's face stained pink at the gesture, but the sparkle in his eyes belied his affection for the young girl whose infectious giggle filled the bakery.

Ada clicked her tongue. "Where'd the time go? I can hardly believe she'll be graduating in a few short weeks." She took a box of assorted pastries from the fridge. "Why don't you get out of here for lunch today and deliver this yourself? You've been working too hard." She set the box on the counter in front of her.

"I still have a tray of tarts to fill." Kara recognized her friend's not-so-subtle suggestion that she walk down the street to the bookstore.

"You know, you're going to feel bad if something happens to the old-timer and you never took the time to properly make amends."

Kara sighed heavily. She'd been thinking the exact same thing earlier when she spotted him using his cane to cross the street. She reached back and untied her apron string, trying to ignore the smirk on Ada's face. "Okay, you win."

She meandered over to the bathroom where she removed her hair net and finger-combed her hair. The dire need of a root touch-up did not go unnoticed. She'd been a redhead all of her life, but the past year or so she'd been fighting a losing battle against the gray and had taken to washing it away once a month.

All in all, she had to admit she wasn't too hard on the eyes. In fact, if she took the time to do her makeup, she looked much younger than her forty years. Not that Abe would notice if she wore any...Noah's alluring smile flashed in her mind and quickened her pulse.

I'm going to have to face him sooner or later.

She scooped the box up from the counter in passing and made a beeline for the front door, stopping to wave to Ada before she stepped outside. The steady lunchtime traffic whizzed by. Maybe he'd be too busy to stop and chat today. It had been some time since she'd bought a new book, not that she needed one. There were at least a dozen volumes she'd yet to read on her home bookshelf, but there was just something about discovering a new title she couldn't resist.

Much to her relief, there were a number of customers in the store. Despite the cluster of people at the cash register, Abe smiled and held up a finger to indicate he'd be with her in a few minutes.

Kara moved right to the romantic suspense section. Her hand flitted from cover to cover. She shivered in the shadow of someone standing behind her. Of course he'd be here helping out through the busy lunch hour. *Where does he work when he's not here?*

"We put the new releases on the shelves beside the front desk now."

His warm breath tickled the back of her neck. A shiver ran down her spine, and she cursed the betrayal of her body.

"Thank you," she replied and scurried toward the cash without a backwards glance. Kara directed her attention to the rows of books—an entire section taken up by the popular romance author, Adam Love. There was something comforting about being amongst all of these books. She'd missed coming here.

"Kara, my dear, I am so glad to see you here." Abe's cheery greeting warmed her heart. He kissed both her cheeks in turn. The bell on the counter sounded and he frowned. "I'm sorry, duty calls."

Kara smiled. "I understand. Here, I thought I'd take a short break and deliver these in person today."

"I wish I could stay and talk." He took the box from her and licked his lips. "Thank you."

"You're very welcome." She watched him walk back to his waiting customers, no trace of discomfort in his gait. *Hmm, that's odd. Why isn't he using his cane?*

"How are you doing, Kara?" Noah appeared out of nowhere.

"Fine. Busy, but fine." She made a concerted effort to remain calm.

"That's good to hear."

"What about you? Everything okay over at Steele Towers?" She regretted saying the words the second they were out of her mouth. She might as well have slapped him across the face given the hurt expression on his face.

He clasped her hand. "Listen, I really haven't had the chance to apologize for my brother's behaviour. I should have told you about placing the order."

"That's the part I don't understand. Why was everything such a big secret?"

"Excuse me, do you work here?" An elderly woman tapped him on the shoulder.

Noah nodded, holding a finger up for Kara's benefit. "I'll just be a minute." His eyes pleaded for Kara to wait. He stooped to listen to the woman, leading her away to another part of the store.

Kara stared blankly at the display of new arrivals, unable to concentrate. *This is going to have to wait for another time*.

Before she left, she caught Abe's attention and pointed to her watch.

He gave her the thumbs up, and she hustled outside. It crossed her mind that Noah might come running up behind her. By the time she made it back to the bakery, she wasn't sure if she felt relieved or disappointed that he hadn't.

Noah saw her leave the bookstore, but his persistent customer demanded his attention while she explained how much romance had changed over the years. At least Kara had visited. That was a good thing.

"It was nice to see Kara today."

Startled, he juggled the stack of books in his arms to keep from dropping them.

"You're wound pretty tight." His grandfather squeezed his arm. "I said it was nice to see Kara today. Too bad we were so busy. I would have liked to have sat down for a proper visit."

"I just hope she understands and doesn't think I was avoiding her questions."

"Maybe you can tell her your side over dinner? I'm sure she takes time to eat now and then. Might I suggest you take her anywhere but Steele Towers?"

"Very funny. Do you think flowers would be overdoing it?"

"You really don't have to. I know you love me." Abe batted his eyelashes.

"Fat lot of help you are."

Abe shook his head. "I can't think of one woman who doesn't like getting flowers. Go ahead and ask her to dinner. What do you have to lose?"

"Oh I don't know, maybe the last of my ego." He put the books on the shelf. "Do you think you'll be okay for a second so I can go across the street to the florist?"

"Go ahead, don't be a chicken, deliver them in person, and ask her out while you're there."

Laughing, Noah left the store. *I can't believe I'm taking romance advice from my grandfather.*

He couldn't remember the last time he'd been inside a flower shop. Floral ambrosia assaulted his senses the moment he stepped inside. He sneezed and walked past an enormous cooler filled with roses. A smaller cooler beside it contained a variety of blooms in a kaleidoscope of colors.

"Can I help you, Mr. Steele?"

Noah shook the owner's hand, surprised he'd called him by name. "Please call me Noah." He pointed to the flowers. "Can you make me a nice arrangement from those? Keep it simple, but pretty."

"Simple but pretty. Can I be so bold to say, as pretty as the lady you are buying them for?"

Noah inwardly cursed the sudden rush of heat to his cheeks. "Yes, she's very pretty. I'll be taking them with me."

"Very good, sir." The decidedly feminine man waved one of his employees over.

Noah strolled down the aisle. Who knew there were so many different kinds of flowers? He hadn't even walked the length of the store before the owner summoned him and presented a cheerful bouquet of pink, red, yellow and white flowers.

"Lots of summer colors here. I hope it meets your approval."

"Yes, it does. Let's hope the lady approves as well."

Outside, he squinted across the road, relieved to find only a couple of customers inside the bakery store front. He stepped out into the street but was forced to stop in mid-stride by a blaring horn. A car came to a screeching halt, far too close for comfort. Noah offered the angry driver an apologetic glance and a friendly wave before jogging over to the curb.

Get a grip, man. He stood in place, breathing nice and slow until his heart stopped racing. *Let's just keep going, shall we?*

The bell above the door jingled, and he stepped inside before coming to a complete stop, awestruck at the sight of the girl serving the customers. There was no denying the young woman was somehow related to Kara. Long auburn hair plaited down her back skimmed the top of her jeans. *She must be Kara's daughter.* Her vivid blue eyes—her mother's eyes—met his.

"Can I help you?" She zeroed in on the flowers he set on the counter and smiled.

"I...I wondered if I might be able to talk to Kara for a minute."

Her eyes sparkled in amusement. "Why don't you go back to the kitchen? I'm sure she'll be happy to see you."

"Let's hope so." He winked and pointed at a set of swinging doors. "There?"

She nodded and smiled. He hoped her mother was half as receptive to him being there.

Kara inspected a tray of vanilla-and-chocolate-swirl cheesecakes she'd just covered with a thin layer of shaved chocolate. She looked up from the tray--her eyes grew big as she took in the beautiful bouquet of flowers. "What's all this?"

"I never had the chance to explain." He set down the flowers on an empty spot next to the cheesecake. "I'd like to take you to supper so we can talk." He noted the confusion in her eyes. "No strings attached. I just want to explain without interruptions."

Silence permeated the kitchen. Finally, she gave in. "Okay, but I must insist on someplace other than Steele Towers."

Her use of his grandfather's *exact* words came as no surprise. "That, I can promise. I'll be by to pick you up...around seven?" He feigned composure, when in reality he wanted to wrap his arms around her and lift her up to meet his lips in a kiss. Seemingly rendered speechless, he tipped two fingers to his forehead in response to her nod and strolled out of the store.

He'd no sooner closed the front door behind him and Joni poked her head in the kitchen, a big grin plastered across her face. "So how long have you been seeing him, and when did you plan on telling me?" She stood with her hands on her hips.

"For the record, I've not been seeing him, or anyone else for that matter. He's the bookstore owner's grandson. He happened to be there a couple of times when I went over to visit Abe."

Joni eyed the floral arrangement suspiciously. "Why the flowers, then? If you're not interested, why are you going out to dinner with him?"

The barrage of questions was growing old fast. "I'll explain everything another time. Let's just say there was a misunderstanding, and he wants to clear the air."

"He totally has a crush on you." Joni smirked as she turned on her heel to leave the kitchen.

Kara grabbed a dishtowel, twisted it, and snapped her daughter's backside. "You're impossible, you know that? Don't you have anything better to do...like, I don't know...work maybe?"

Joni disappeared through the swinging doors in a fit of

giggles.

Sometimes she's still very much a little girl.

Chapter Six

Kara hoped to finish work a little early, but as luck would have it, she ended up doing the mad dash to get ready for her dinner with Noah. There wasn't time to second-guess her choice of outfit. Not that she was a social butterfly and had a separate wardrobe for her nights out on the town. In fact, the last time she went out to eat probably consisted of dinner at Denny's with Joni.

Basic black dress slacks and a simple white linen blouse would have to suffice. She towel-dried her mass of fiery red hair and left it hanging down her back. Kara slipped the blouse over the best of her sad-looking bras. She remembered reading somewhere that the best way to assure you don't sleep with a man on the first date is not to shave your legs and to wear the ugliest bra and panty set you own..

"Better than birth control." She snapped the strap of her bra and buttoned her blouse. *What the hell am I thinking of birth control for? I have no desire to enter the Steele circle. I agreed to dinner for Abe's sake, didn't I?*

Her feet slipped easily into a pair of black sling backs that Joni had loaned her. She walked through a spray of her favourite perfume, just as the doorbell rang.

Ready or not, here I come.

Kara opened the door to reveal a very handsome Noah Steele dressed in casual slacks and a pale blue button-down shirt opened enough to reveal the smooth skin of what looked to be a broad, firm chest. His blond hair was back in its usual ponytail, the perfect complement to his olive complexion. Much to her delight, he seemed to be as nervous as she felt. Perspiration beaded his forehead as he feasted his eyes on her, his rigid expression changing into a warm smile.

"You look lovely." He clasped her hands and drew her to him, lightly kissing her cheeks. The combination of him and the scent of his musky cologne left her breathless.

"You clean up pretty nice yourself."

Noah offered his arm, and she slipped a hand in the crook, allowing him to usher her to a sleek little silver sports car—a not-so-gentle reminder of his status in life.

"I hope you don't mind us taking my father's car. Mine is in the shop."

Kara wasn't sure how she should reply, so she opted to say nothing. Sitting in the low riding machine was a little intimidating. To say she felt like a fish out of water would be putting it mildly.

"I'm glad you agreed to have dinner with me, Kara."

She smiled. "So where are you taking me?"

"I hope you like seafood. There's a great place right on the water."

"I love seafood." Her words came out faster than intended. *Get a grip!*

The car glided through town as if it were floating on air. She noticed a few heads turn and nod in approval. They drove alongside the lake. The moon reflected off of the water, illuminating the boats in the harbour. The car slowed and turned in the parking lot. She didn't ever remember seeing a restaurant down here. Noah parked next to the dock.

"Here we are." He winked and got out, rounding the front of the car and opening her door.

What the hell is going on? There wasn't a restaurant in sight. "I don't understand." She searched his face, curious about the glint in his eyes.

"You will in a minute." He took her hand and led her down the dock to a rather impressive boat. Hundreds of twinkling white lights adorned the deck. "It's the perfect night for a cruise around the harbour. We'll be having dinner on board."

"You're kidding, right?" Was she out of her mind? Getting on a boat to God knows where with a man she had trust issues with?

Sensing her reluctance, he held both of her hands and stared intently into her eyes. "Listen, Kara, I just wanted to take you someplace where we wouldn't be hovered over because of my last name. Contrary to what you might believe, I don't bask in the Steele spotlight. As you can see, I go to great lengths to avoid it."

Kara not only did she see the sincerity in his eyes, she actually felt it. *I should probably run away and not look back.* Before she had the chance to talk herself out of going on the cruise, he led her to the heart of the boat where a simple yet elegant table for two had been set for them.

A man in a crisp white uniform entered the room. "If you're ready, we'll push off Mr. Steele."

"Very good."

"Is everything always so formal, Mr. Steele?" Kara sat down on the chair he pulled out for her.

He laughed. "Hardly." Noah sat across the table from her. "In fact, this is probably only the third or fourth time I've been on this boat since I was a kid."

"It really is beautiful. I can't imagine having a boat like this and not wanting to use it."

Noah's twinkling brown eyes clouded. "Trust me, being a Steele isn't everything you might think. People treat you differently, and it has nothing to do with you as a person."

"Is that the real reason you and your grandfather kept the fact you're Steele's from me?"

Another man wearing a similar uniform entered the room brandishing a bottle of wine. He stood at the side of the table and poured a small amount in Noah's glass. Noah swirled the amber liquid before taking a small sip and nodding his approval. The steward filled both their glasses and left them alone.

"Thank you." She clinked his glass with hers and took a tentative sip. It was unlike any wine she'd ever tasted. A medley of fruit flavours exploded in her mouth. "Mmm, this is good."

"To answer your question, we didn't necessarily keep anything from you, at least not intentionally. I guess we've just grown accustomed to presenting ourselves as just that, ourselves—normal."

"I guess I can understand that, although the part about getting me a gig at Steele Towers all seemed a little secretive, don't you think?"

"I admit, I might have gone about it the wrong way. For that I am truly sorry. My grandfather went on and on about your desserts, and when I tried them for myself, I knew your talent deserved to be in the spotlight. The doctors' conference just happened to offer the perfect opportunity."

Kara sighed. Everything he said made sense. Maybe it wasn't so much about Abe and his hand in it all. Maybe it was more an issue of not being in control. Could her reaction be as simple as a defence mechanism?

She raised her glass. "Truce?"

Noah visibly relaxed and returned her smile. "Truce."

The boat slipped away from the dock.

"I can't believe we're actually on a boat. I'm afraid I've only been on much smaller boats, where life jackets were mandatory as was hanging on for dear life," she said.

"Would you like to go up on deck? The view really is spectacular at night. Marcus will let us know when dinner is served."

The deck offered a magnificent view of the glittering city lights. She'd imagined their dinner together would be memorable, but never in her wildest dreams did she think she'd be dining aboard a private yacht on the St. Lawrence Seaway. A slight breeze lifted the hair from her neck. Not a ripple or another boat for as far as the eye could see.

"Did you reserve the whole river?"

Noah chuckled. "Not even a Steele has that much power."

Kara remembered her doctor greeting Joni's arrival into the world. *Welcome to Brockville, Home of a Thousand Islands.* The harbour yawned open to a stupendous glass pool. She welcomed the fresh air and took a deep cleansing breath.

They stood in silence under a canopy of twinkling stars. In the background, the sultry tones of a romantic sax serenade. It seemed he'd gone to a lot of trouble for a dinner and he'd promised no strings attached. Kara caught a glimpse of his profile. He gazed out over the beauty that surrounded them, as hers remained transfixed on the beauty beside her. She'd never used the word beautiful to describe a man before. The moon illuminated his flawless skin, not even a trace of stubble so many men got soon after they'd shaved. Once again, she resisted the urge to release his hair from the pony tail.

"Do you approve?"

The huskiness of his voice set every nerve ending in her body on high alert. She dropped her gaze, feigning interest in her hands on the railing..

Noah placed a finger under her chin and lifted her face so she was forced to look at him. "Why can't you look at me?"

What she saw in his eyes robbed her of breath. Before she could utter a word, he dipped down and gently covered her lips with his own. The softness of his touch surprised her.

He stepped back and matched the intensity of her gaze. In that moment, they were the only two people in existence. He kissed her again, this time with a sense of urgency. Her body responded and melded to his firm chest. A groan erupted from deep within him, and she gasped.

Someone cleared their throat behind them, interrupting the intense moment. "Pardon me for the interruption, but dinner is served," Marcus announced.

Kara welcomed the timely interruption. She broke free of Noah's hold and turned toward the dining room. "I'm starved. Shall we go?" she said, breathlessly.

Both of their wine glasses had been topped off, and Kara took a healthy swallow before she sat down. She slipped her trembling hand from the stem of the wine glass to her lap. Noah gave her the time needed to gather her composure. He'd never planned on the kiss, but he wasn't sorry it happened. Making Kara uncomfortable definitely wasn't on his agenda.

Kara took her fork in hand and seemed to be having trouble deciding how to approach the colourful salad.

"It's almost too pretty to eat, isn't it?"

She tittered nervously. "I'd say so. It seems a shame to

disrupt it in any way."

Noah smiled and stabbed a forkful, popping it in his mouth. "Mmm, I can vouch it tastes even better than it looks."

She followed suit, her rigid posture visibly relaxed. "I don't think I've ever had a salad quite like this."

"Then I'm glad I talked the estate chef to cook for us tonight."

"Do you mean to tell me, someone...a chef, cooks your meals for you?"

Amused, he dabbed the corners of his mouth. "I'm afraid, in our wing of the estate, we mostly fend for ourselves. Occasionally, or on a night like tonight, Chef welcomes the change in scenery."

Kara finished her salad and drained the last of her wine. She'd just set her empty glass down and Marcus appeared at the table, refilled their glasses, and took their empty plates away. She followed everything that happened with the wide-eyed wonder of a child, reminding Noah just how different their worlds were.

"Did you grow up around here?" asked Noah.

Her smile faded, and he regretted the question.

She sighed. "My family lives in Ottawa. I left home at sixteen and have never been back. Joni was actually born at Brockville General; we lived in the country most of her life."

The mention of Joni brought the smile back to her face. He took the hint, and steered the conversation away from her roots. "Joni seems to be a good girl. She looks like you."

Kara beamed. "I'll take that as a compliment. Joni is my world. I couldn't ask for a better daughter."

Marcus entered the room, followed by the waiter. Each of them brandished a platter of mouth-watering seafood. Once they set the food down, Marcus lit a flame under a small metal chafing dish filled with garlic butter.

"Oh dear, so much for counting calories tonight." Kara rubbed her hands together and laughed.

"Good. Maybe it can make up for the oodles of calories we've consumed since discovering your cheesecake."

She skewered a chunk of lobster. "Touché." She swirled it in garlic butter and popped it in her mouth. She closed her eyes.

"Oh, my lord...I think I've died and gone to Heaven."

Noah stared transfixed by a trail of butter slowly dripping down her chin. He imagined leaning over the table and following the trail with the tip of his tongue."

"Are you okay?" Kara searched his eyes.

Noah cleared his throat and squirmed in his chair. The warmth of his cheeks made him grateful for the dimly lit room. "I'm fine."

"Excuse me sir." Marcus stood in the doorway. The seriousness to his tone commanded Noah's full attention. "I'm afraid we must turn around and head for shore immediately."

"What seems to be the problem?" Annoyed, Noah wiped his mouth on a napkin.

"If I could speak to you in private, sir."

Noah shook his head. "I'm sorry for the interruption, Kara." He balled up his cloth napkin and tossed it on his plate. "I'll just be a moment."

The sexual tension between them quickly dissipated.

Noah joined Marcus and closed the door behind him. "What's this all about?"

"I'm afraid it's your brother."

"Caleb?" His temperature rose.

"Yes, sir. I received a message from harbour control. It seems your brother reported unauthorized use of the boat. We must return to the dock or the authorities will be paying us a visit."

"You've got to be joking. Didn't you tell them it's me here on the boat?"

Marcus shrugged. "It seems you didn't follow proper procedure. They have no way of knowing you are who you say you are."

"Just wait until I get my hands on him. Follow the harbour masters' instructions. I'll have to deal with this in person."

Noah took a deep breath in an effort to mask his anger. Caleb had gone too far as usual. *What kind of games is he playing this time?* He dreaded having to cut his time with Kara short.

Kara now stood at the glass wall, looking out over the water.

She turned to face him. “Is everything okay?”

“Nothing for you to worry about, but I’m afraid we must return to shore.” He cursed the confusion that clouded her captivating blue eyes. He better come clean with her. “It seems my little brother has struck again.”

“What do you mean?”

“Caleb is big on proper procedure, and I didn’t follow the rules when I took the boat.”

“Isn’t this your family’s boat? You mean to tell me you can’t use it whenever you want to?”

“I guess you’ve figured out we’re not your typical warm-and-fuzzy family. For every luxury at our disposal, there is a price to pay in order to use it.”

“I’m beginning to understand your reluctance to be linked to the name. Unfortunately, the Steele reputation precedes you, and there’s not much you can do about that.”

Truer words were never spoken. He wiped his mouth and swallowed the last half of his glass of wine. His little brother’s timing couldn’t be worse. Kara had just started to relax and enjoy herself.

“If it’s okay with you, I’d like to go up on deck for the trip back to the harbour.” She picked up her wine glass from the table.

“We still have time to finish our meal.” He perused the mountain of food still left untouched.

“I’m sorry, Noah. It was all so very wonderful. Really, it was, but I seem to have lost my appetite.”

“If you insist, of course we can go up.” He struggled to keep his anger at his brother in check.

“You’re not mad at me, are you?”

Noah shook his head and refilled his glass. “Not in the least; it’s not you I’m angry with.” He took her by the hand and led her up on deck.

“Caleb knows you’re out here, doesn’t he?” Kara stood at the railing and looked out on the water.

“He sure does.” Noah gritted his teeth.

“Why would he do something like this to you?”

Noah hated the turn their evening together had taken. "Because he can...and because it's his not-so-subtle reminder of the rules. He's a bit of a control freak when my father's not around."

Kara turned and gazed into his eyes. "I'm sorry."

Noah joined her at the railing and slipped an arm around her waist. "You have nothing to be sorry about. How about we just enjoy the ride back without talking about my little brother?"

Kara tapped his glass with hers. "Deal." She eased against his side and gazed out upon the still waters.

All too soon, the lights from the harbour broke the amiable silence between them, and her sigh pierced his heart. *Caleb is going to pay dearly for this one.* The yacht eased up to the dock where a small group of men with badges on their shirtsleeves awaited their arrival.

"What happens now?" asked Kara.

"Now, I'm going to ask these gentlemen if I can take you home before we discuss any of this." He escorted her to a deck chair. "Wait here and I'll see what I can do."

Kara smiled in a futile attempt to hide her obvious disappointment.

"Mr. Steele, I presume?" The tallest of the three men extended his hand. "I'm sorry about all of this, but I have to follow orders."

"I understand." He shook the officer's hand. "As you can see, I'm in the company of a lovely young lady. Would you allow me to take her home before we sort this all out?"

The officer turned his attention to the parking lot. "I assume that's the car you intended on using?"

Noah watched a tow truck back up to his father's car."Aw, shit! Let me guess, Caleb?"

"I'm afraid it's been reported stolen."

Noah looked back at the yacht to find Kara walking toward him. He threw up his hands in frustration. "I can't believe this is happening, Kara. He reported my father's car stolen too!"

Kara shook her head and kissed his cheek. "It's not your fault.

Point me in the direction of a phone and I'll call a taxi."

"I hate this." He frowned, and gave her his cell phone.

She smiled and winked at him. "You owe me a dinner."

Noah cracked a smile. *What a woman.* "You, my dear, have a date."

Chapter Seven

"The dynamics of that family are confusing to say the least." Kara peered over her coffee cup at her daughter.

Joni popped the last wedge of toast in her mouth and brushed the crumbs from her fingers. "It seems to me that Noah says he doesn't want to be judged by his Steele name, but he still uses the perks that come with it whenever it's to his advantage."

Kara shrugged. "And royally pisses his little brother off in the process."

"Why does Caleb get so bent out of shape over things?"

"I think it's because Caleb's life revolves around making his father proud and keeping the Steele Empire running smoothly. All of a sudden, big brother steps in and throws everything off kilter by doing things with little regard for protocol."

"I'll take our simple life any day." Joni pecked Kara on the forehead before leaving the kitchen to change for work.

Kara sipped her coffee, still trying to process the events of her date with Noah. There was no denying the chemistry between them. Never had a kiss affected her so deeply. Her troubled marriage left her more than a little gun-shy when it came to relationships. Did she really want to become emotionally vested in a man like Noah? Could she be involved with him and keep detached from his toxic sibling rivalry? How did Abe stay removed from the Steele insanity? He'd built a thriving business without using the Steele name. What exactly did Noah do when he wasn't helping his grandfather?

She pushed back from the table and grimaced. Her body resisted every movement as if she'd pulled an all-nighter. Tossing and turning didn't help any. It would be a very long day.

"Mom, you better get moving or we're going to miss the bus."

Kara trudged upstairs. "When did we change roles around

here?"

Joni came out of her room fully dressed, her skin radiant. She pulled Kara up the few remaining steps. "I am leaving work at lunch to pick up my dress. I can hardly wait for you to see it."

"I'm sure you'll be gorgeous in it." Kara still felt a little guilty about not helping her pay for it, but Joni insisted she would buy it on her own.

"Now we just have to go dress shopping for you." She pushed Kara into her bedroom. "I'll be waiting downstairs."

Kara scrunched up her face at her reflection in the mirror. *Dress shopping*. The last time she'd bought a fancy dress, she'd got married in it. She'd worn a long white lace dress, and he'd been so handsome in his tails, top hat and blue jeans. They were so carefree back then. *When did it all gone so terribly wrong?*

"Ten minutes, Mom!"

"Shit!" Kara pulled her nightgown up over her head and slipped into blue jeans and t-shirt, fumbling with the button on her jeans as she dashed down the stairs. She hated being rushed—it usually threw her off kilter for the rest of the day.

Joni had set out her slip on shoes and held out her purse. "You're never this late."

"See what happens when you let a man into your headspace?" She wagged a finger at her daughter and snatched her purse. "No good can come of it, I tell you...."

As expected, the day dragged out painfully. Fred suggested she go home early a number of times, but Kara refused. Why should they carry her workload because of her own stupidity? Besides, she'd noticed over the past couple of weeks, Fred had started to really show his age. He'd taken to going home right after the morning bread orders were filled, whereas he usually liked to hang about and talk it up with the customers.

Shortly after he'd left for the day, Kara passed the office and noticed Ada sitting behind her desk with her head in her hands. She stepped inside as quietly as possible; concern drove her to Ada's side. "Is everything okay?"She put a hand on her shoulder.

Ada's body trembled beneath it.

Her heavy sigh filled the room, and Kara waited patiently for a reply. It was so out of character for Ada.

"Please, sit down, Kara."

It broke her heart to see such sadness in her dear friends' eyes. *Something is terribly wrong.*

"I'm going to ask you to keep what I'm about to tell you to yourself." She dabbed at her eyes with a crumpled tissue she took from the arm of her shirt.

"Of course."

"I'm sure you've noticed a change in Fred of late."

Her eyes filled with moisture. *Oh my God, this can't be good.*

Ada drew a shaky breath. "I'm afraid it's bad news...." Her voice cracked.

Kara made a move to go to her friend, but she held up a hand to stop her.

"Please, let me finish."

Her stomach churned, scared shitless to hear what came next.

Ada straightened in her chair. "Fred has cancer." Her mouth set in a grim line.

"How bad is it?" *Cancer? There has to be some kind of mistake. Why is this happening to him?*

"Bad, it's inoperable." Ada buried her face in her hands, her body wracked with sobs.

Kara shook her head in disbelief. "This can't be true. Surely there's something that can be done...chemotherapy?"

"No, it's too late for any of that. There's nothing to do...but wait." She laid her head on her desk and gave in to her heartbreak.

Kara hurried to her side, gathering her into her arms. Indescribable pain consumed her. *This is so unfair.*

Fred was one of the most giving, most caring men she'd ever known. He alone kept the hope alive there were still good men in the world.

A knock at the door separated the two women. They both

wiped at their eyes and straightened their clothes.

"Remember your promise," Ada pleaded.

She walked over to the door, and rather than let Joni in, slipped out to join her.

"I'm sorry to interrupt," Joni apologized. "I really need to be going to pick up my dress."

Kara noted the curious way her daughter looked at her.

She waved her away. "Of course, you go on." Kara quickly walked out to the cash. A number of customers were in the store. Joni stood behind her.

"Is everything okay?" Joni whispered in her ear.

"Yes, I'm just overtired. Don't you worry about a thing and get going."

"Are you sure?"

Kara gathered every ounce of strength she had within her and feigned a smile. She turned to Joni and brushed a kiss on her cheek. "Very sure, now get on with you."

Thankfully, a customer came to the cash to keep any further questions at bay. Kara knew her daughter, and she wasn't buying any of it.

Joni gathered her things. "I'll see you at home this evening. We'll talk then."

Kara shook her head and smiled at her elderly customer. "Kids."

The door to the office remained closed for the rest of the afternoon, and a steady stream of customers kept her busy. She forced all thoughts from her mind and handled the store on her own. She was beyond exhaustion, physically and emotionally, by the time she flipped the sign in the window to CLOSED.

Ada finally emerged, freshened up since Kara left her, but still appeared distraught and very tired.

Ada took hold of her hands. "You have to promise me something."

Her boss looked more serious than she'd ever seen her.

"Of course, name it."

"You mustn't tell a soul about any of this." She squeezed her hands. "Fred doesn't want anyone to know, especially not you and Joni."

"I don't know if I can. How can I face him without him knowing that I know?"

"You'll find a way." She firmed her hold and stared intently into Kara's eyes. "You have to."

Kara briefly closed her eyes and drew a ragged breath. *Am I strong enough to pull this off?* She sighed resignedly. "I will try."

Chapter Eight

Noah hadn't talked to Kara since their date of sorts. A couple of days ago, she'd passed him in front of the bookstore without acknowledging his presence. He even called out to her, and she completely ignored him. He didn't think there was any point in trying to contact her after that. Maybe he didn't have the right to. If he cared for her at all, he'd keep her far away from the dysfunctional Steele family.

To make matters worse, his father was due home from abroad. Normally this wouldn't make any difference to Noah's life in anyway, but Caleb would be sure to make it a problem this time. He never missed an opportunity to make himself look good, and he'd undoubtedly put a spin on the events of late to do just that. No, there would be no avoiding the family meeting this time.

Family meeting.

A wave of dread washed over him. His chest tightened, the same way it always did at the mention of being in his father's presence. Not much had changed since the first meeting he could remember. His father's desk didn't look quite as big as it did when he was a child. He'd still be greeted with a firm handshake, unless, of course, the reason for the meeting was of a more serious nature. If this were the case, he'd remain seated behind his ominous wood desk.

The meeting he remembered most took place shortly after his mother took sick. His father announced that his mother would be moving to a facility where she would receive the care she needed. For the first time in his life, he'd stood up to his father. He threatened to go public if he didn't agree to let them move into the west wing where he would be solely responsible for his mother's care.

"I'll agree to this under one condition...you will tell no one of this," his father's eyes narrowed, and turned black as night, "and I mean *no one*."

Since that day, neither Caleb nor his father had set foot in the west wing. Noah squeezed his eyes shut, forcing the memory from his mind. His hand smoothed over the glossy finish of the book in his hand.

"Noah?"

"Huh?" His eyes sprung open, and he lost his grip on the book. "I'm right here, Gramps." He retrieved the volume from the floor, inspecting the binding for damage.

"Your father has sent a car for you." Curiosity filled his milky eyes. "What's up?"

Noah sighed wearily and placed the book on the shelf. "Family meeting."

Abe shook his head. "You have nothing to worry about."

He shrugged. "You're probably right, but that's not going to stop me from doing exactly that."

"Maybe he just wants to touch base after being gone so long."

"I highly doubt that."Noah sneered. "I'm sure Caleb has filled his head with all sorts of bullshit."

Abe walked him to the door. "Do you want me to come with you?"

Noah squeezed his grandfather's shoulder. "Thanks, but there's not much sense in ruining both of our days." He opened the door and stepped outside. "Wish me luck."

"Good morning, Noah." Jeffery, his father's butler, personal valet, and one-man show, greeted him outside of his father's office.

"Good morning, Jeffery."

"Your father and brother are waiting." He stepped aside. If he had any knowledge of the nature of this meeting, his stony demeanour gave nothing away.

Caleb sat in his usual place across from his father. He looked straight ahead without acknowledging his arrival.

"Thank you for coming." Zachary Steele remained seated.

One would never guess he'd not seen his children for several months.

"You look well, Father." Noah took the empty seat beside his brother.

"Let's get right to the point, shall we?" His long fingers formed a steeple under his chin. "I understand you hired a certain young lady to cater the desserts for one of our events?"

"Yes, but I assure—"

Zachary Steele held up his hand to halt his response. "I've received a number of phone calls about these desserts." He opened and closed his fingers. "I want her."

"Pardon me?"

"I want her in the Steele Kitchens. Can you make this happen? Caleb seems to think you're the man for the job."

Caleb shrunk down in his chair.

You can't be serious. "I doubt if Ms. Walker is interested in leaving the bakery."

"Everyone has a price. Have you learned nothing from me?"

Noah grimaced at his father's condescending tone. "Not everyone." He held his father's steely gaze.

"I don't have time for this. I will expect an answer by the morning." He stood up behind his desk, ending the discussion. "I'm rather tired."

Noah stifled the urge to fire a scathing retort at his father. Arguing with him was futile. If he didn't have a chat with Kara, he'd send one of his bloodsucking associates to try and coerce her. His father left the room, and he turned to face his brother.

"I suppose I have you to thank for this?" The sight of him cowering in his chair sickened him.

Caleb straightened. "What's the big deal? Go make the lady an offer she can't refuse."

"For the record, little brother, not everyone can be bought."

"Well, if you don't think you can convince her, I'd be happy to try." Caleb stood, sporting an over-confident smirk.

Noah jumped to his feet, standing no more than an inch from his brother's face. "You stay the hell away from Kara."

Caleb stepped back with his hands up, protecting his *pretty* face. “Not a problem, as long as you do as Father asks.” He strolled across the office, and stopped at the door. “It’s been a pleasure, as always, big brother.” The corners of his mouth lifted in a twisted smile, and he ducked out into the hallway.

“Son of a....” Noah clenched his fists. He hated being forced to go to Kara with an offer. He sighed and rubbed his jaw.

Does everyone really have a price?

Chapter Nine

Never in Kara's life had it been so difficult to keep a reign on her emotions. It was two days until Joni's graduation, and it took every ounce of her self-control to keep Fred's secret until the big day passed. Fred hadn't been to work since Ada told her of the cancer. As far as he knew, everyone thought he'd come down with a bad case of the flu, and under no circumstances was anyone to visit him. The last thing he wanted was for everyone to get sick.

"Do you think Fred will be well enough to come to my graduation?" Joni asked Ada as she put a batch of bread in the ovens.

"I don't know, dear. You know how much he wants to be there, don't you?"

Joni kissed her flushed cheek. "Of course I do. I thought I'd have a friend video tape it for him. Do you think he'd like that?"

Kara watched her boss struggle to maintain her composure. She pulled Joni into her warm embrace and kissed her cheek. "He would love that," she replied, her voice thick with emotion.

"Is that the last batch?" Kara butted in, hoping to save her friend from the emotional exchange. Over the past few days, she'd often wondered how much more Ada could take without breaking down.

Ada pulled away from Joni and set the timer. "Yes, how about a cup of coffee before we start filling today's orders?"

Kara wiped her hands on the front of her apron. "That sounds lovely."

"You two go ahead. I'll keep an eye on things." Joni balanced a tray of apple strudel to fill the front showcase.

"You're a godsend." *Thank God I have you, Joni.*

Joni beamed under her mother's praise and disappeared through the swinging doors.

Kara ushered her frazzled friend to the front doors. "Go out to the bench. I'll bring the coffee."

Without argument, she slipped outside. From the window she watched her plop down and close her eyes. Kara's heart ached for her friend. *There must be something more I can do to take some of the burden from her shoulders.* She wasn't a young woman any more, and wouldn't be able to keep this pace up for much longer. They needed to hire extra help; it was that simple.

She filled their mugs and brought them outside where they sat in amiable silence before Kara spoke up. "Ada, do you trust me?"

Ada's brow knit. "Of course I do. Why do you ask?"

"I want to help, but I need you to trust me."

"What do you have in mind?"

Kara took a deep breath. "I think you need to be home with Fred."

She sighed wearily and dabbed at her eyes. "That's simply not an option. There's far too much to do here."

"Why don't you let me run the place until Fred is feeling better?"

"You can't do all of this on your own."

"I wouldn't be doing it on my own. I have Joni, and I know she has a couple of friends who need a summer job."

"I don't know." She shook her head.

"Let me ask the twins to come in tomorrow so you can meet them." She squeezed Ada's hand. "At least give it a try. If you make yourself sick you won't be any good to Fred, never mind running a bakery."

Resignation filled her tired eyes. The corners of her mouth lifted in the first semblance of a smile in days. "Yes, I'll give it a try." She put an arm across Kara's back and pulled her against her side. "I love you, Kara. You're the daughter I always prayed for."

"And you're the mother that actually wanted me."

Noah stepped out of the bookstore fully intending to walk down to the bakery and make Kara an offer she couldn't refuse. That is, until he saw the heartfelt exchange between the two women. *There's no way she's going to leave the bakery; it doesn't matter how much money is involved.*

He'd been up most of the night trying to figure out how he was going to get Kara to accept his father's offer to come to the Steele Kitchens. Kara didn't strike him as the type of woman who could be bought. In fact, she'd probably be insulted. If he didn't succeed, his father would undoubtedly try his iron-man tactics. There must be some way to convince him to just leave her alone.

"Are you coming in or going out?" Abe squeezed by him, and looked in the same direction as him to the bench in front of the bakery.

"Sorry, I guess I got distracted."

"And what a lovely distraction she is." Abe winked.

Heat rushed to Noah's face.

Abe slapped his back. "Oh boy! You've really got it bad."

Noah scowled. "You don't know what you're talking about, old man."

He cupped his warm cheek with a cool hand. "Any woman who can make a man blush without saying a word...." He snickered.

Noah didn't even bother defending himself; it was futile to try. There was also no denying how the lovely Kara Walker got under his skin like no other woman ever had.

"So how was your father's trip abroad?"

Noah followed his grandfather inside. "How the hell would I know?"

The tiny worry lines around Abe's wise, old eyes deepened. He kneeled down beside a box of books and opened it.

"I'm sorry. You know your son; he's not into idle chit chat."

"Then why did he call a family meeting?"

Noah stood in the doorway, his attention drifted to the now-empty bench in front of the bakery. "He wants Kara."

Abe's eyes grew big. "What?"

His grandfather's misinterpretation of his words brought the slightest of smiles to his mouth. "Not in that way. He wants her to come over to the Steele side and work in the Kitchens."

He rubbed his temples. "Let me guess: he wants you to convince her. Everybody's got a price, right?"

"You got it." His father used the expression quite often discussing business.

"I'm sorry." Abe used Noah's shoulder to push himself up on his feet. "Some things never change. What Zachary wants, Zachary gets, but with no regard for anyone but himself."

"That's what I'm afraid of."

"Not to change the subject, but a little bird told me young Joni is graduating this weekend. Why don't you send your father a memo and tell him you'll do what he asks after the weekend? It's not a solution, but it should buy you a little more time."

"Thanks. I guess a little more time is better than nothing. Maybe I can think of a way out of this whole mess by then."

Noah recognized the familiar yet sad expression on his grandfather's face as he carried a stack of books to the counter. There was nothing he could say to change his father's mind, but he'd be damned if he'd stand idly by and watch the vultures swoop down on Kara. For the second time in his life he was going to stand up to his father, no matter what detriment it meant for him.

Chapter Ten

Fred's phone call the previous night to thank Kara pulled her from her bed seconds before the alarm sounded at four. Still half asleep, she wrestled with her clothes and hurried downstairs. True to his word, Tyler sat outside the apartment at exactly four-twenty.

Thank God I don't have to take the bus.

Tyler opened the door from inside the cab and smiled broadly. "Good morning, boss." He waited for her to buckle her seat belt before handing her a coffee.

"We're going to get along just fine." Kara gratefully accepted the hot brew and inhaled its heavenly aroma.

He laughed. "Joni warned me you need your caffeine fix in the morning."

"She's a smart girl."

"So, do you really think I can make bread?"

"You'll do fine. It's much easier than it used to be. The machines do most of the work. As long as you know the difference between flour and salt, we should be good to go."

Tyler's big brown eyes sparkled with anticipation, reminding Kara of how she'd felt the first day on the job. She couldn't be happier that Ada had fallen for the twins' charm and agreed to hire them. Both boys stood over six feet tall with a mass of chocolate brown curls. They were good kids, and she looked forward to working with them.

It felt strange coming to work and not having Ada and Fred to greet her. She turned the key in the lock and rushed over to disable the alarm. Until now, she'd never registered just how much work they actually did. Luckily, Tyler was a quick study, and in no time, they worked together as smoothly as a well-oiled machine.

Tyler's eyes lit up at seeing the first batch of bread come out of the ovens. He hovered over the golden-brown crusts and inhaled deeply.

"You're a natural." Kara put another batch of bread in the oven. "Come over here and I'll show you how to separate the dough to make buns."

Teaching Tyler kept her mind off the fact Ada and Fred weren't there. With graduation in only two days, she couldn't wait to hear of Fred's reaction when he found out they were taping the ceremony for him.

The twins agreed to set up the equipment before they dressed for the event. All they were told was that Fred was too sick to attend. They already knew Joni thought of him as her grandfather.

The bells on the front door tinkled, signalling Joni and Tyson's arrival. Tyson stifled a laugh upon seeing his brother covered in flour and dividing the dough in sections for buns. "We definitely have to get a picture of this."

Tyler blew a palm filled with flour at his unsuspecting brother's face.

"Hey!"

The four of them laughed in unison. Fred and Ada would be thrilled to hear laughter in the bakery again.

"You two get ready to work." Kara winked. Her smile quickly faded upon seeing Caleb Steele in the doorway, a phony smile plastered on his clean-shaven face.

"Good morning, Ms. Walker. I wondered if I might have a moment of your time." He looked down his narrow nose at Joni as she walked past him. "Alone."

Kara wasn't in the mood to talk to the likes of him. He was on her territory now. "I'm afraid you picked a bad time. Perhaps if you call later in the day, I'll try to pencil you in at *my* convenience."

Caleb's jaw dropped and snapped shut just as quickly. "It will only take a minute, and I think you will want to hear what I have to say."

"I can't imagine you having anything I want to hear, but if you insist, I'll set aside a few minutes during my lunch hour." She drove her fist into a mound of dough. "Take it, or leave it."

Kara noted the struggle going on for him to control his temper. "I'll be back at twelve. Good day." He spun on his heel to leave.

"Make that 12:15."

He stopped in his tracks, and rolled back his shoulders. "As you wish," he replied without looking back.

"Mom! Could you have been ruder?"

Kara burst out laughing. "Trust me, he's lucky I didn't kick his pompous ass out the door."

"Who is he?"

"Caleb Steele. Someone you don't want to know."

Joni chuckled. "I've never heard you talk that way to anyone. If you feel that way, why did you agree to meet with him?"

"You don't think I actually plan of being here when he shows up, do you?"

"You wouldn't!"

The shocked look on her daughter's face was priceless. "I absolutely would, and I will."

Joni shook her head.

"Now let's get busy, we have a lot of work to do this morning." Kara imagined Caleb would be none too happy to learn how much pleasure their little exchange of words brought to her.

Sorry about your luck, Mr. Steele. If you plan on using your bullying tactics, you've messed with the wrong girl.

Noah thanked the weather gods for the sudden downpour. The rain slowed business down to a trickle, and brought Kara to the front door, where she shook out her umbrella before stepping inside the store.

"What a nice surprise." Abe smiled from behind the cash. "To what do we owe this honor?"

Kara put a finger to her lips and giggled. "Shh, I'm hiding."

Abe's eyes sparkled in amusement. "You are, are you? And

who from, pray tell?"

Kara peeked out from behind the display in the window to watch the front door of the bakery. "From your grandson."

Noah frowned and stepped out from an aisle of books. "Sorry to ruin your fun, but I'm right here."

Color rushed to her cheeks. "Oh dear." She giggled again. "I meant the other one, Caleb."

Relief washed over him, quickly replaced by panic. *What in the hell is Caleb up to?* "Why would you be hiding from my brother?"

Kara repeated the conversation exchanged between them that morning. "I can't imagine what he has to say to me, but you can bet your ass I'm not going to make it easy for him."

Abe slapped his knee. "That's my girl!"

"There he is." Kara waved them to the window.

Caleb stepped out of the limo, under the umbrella his chauffer held out for him. He straightened his jacket with an air of self-importance. If Kara wasn't standing next to him, he would have bolted from the store and picked him up by his perfectly creased lapels. *Is my dear brother acting on his own initiative or on our father's orders?*

"Who's working today?" asked Noah.

"Don't worry. Joni can more than handle the likes of him." She snorted.

"She shouldn't have to. You two stay here."

Before either had a chance to respond, he darted out the front door. He shoved his hands in the front pockets of his jeans and acted as if he were going for a leisurely stroll despite the rain. He reached the corner of the bakery just as Caleb swung open the door and stormed out. If he hadn't noticed him, they would have collided.

Caleb's expression switched from anger to fear. "I, uh, just wanted to pick up some pastries for father."

Noah's gaze dropped to Caleb's empty hands, and he raised a brow.

"They were out of cinnamon buns, so I ordered a mixture to

be delivered."

"And you couldn't place an order by phone? Or, did you just happen to be in the neighbourhood?"

Caleb squirmed under his scrutiny, flipping up the collar of his jacket in a futile attempt to shield himself from the rain. "I could ask you the same thing, big brother. What are you doing here?"

"You forget, dear brother, I spend time every day with *our* grandfather, and Ms. Walker is our friend."

"Of course, how is Grandfather?"

Noah had to laugh at his brother's attempt to change the subject. He could care less about his grandfather. "You know, I can't help but wonder if there isn't another reason for your visit to the bakery. Perhaps I need to talk to Father. I don't recall him asking for you to take care of things."

"Well, since you haven't done anything about it, I thought I'd try to talk to her."

Noah stepped forward until he was a mere whisper from his brother's overly bright eyes. "I'm going to give you a suggestion" He ran his fingers down the crease of his wet lapels. "You let me take care of any business with Ms. Walker. I tend to be very protective of my friends, something you know nothing about."

"I'll leave." His jaw clenched.

Noah relaxed his hold, and Caleb escaped to the safety of the limo. Once inside, he lowered the window half way. "Rest assured, if you don't take care of things, I'll be back."

Noah stared intensely into his brother's eyes. "I promise, if you do...I'll be waiting."

Caleb nodded curtly at his driver, and the limo slipped away down the street. Footsteps approached him from behind. He turned to find Abe and Kara under an umbrella.

"You're going to catch your death standing here in the rain."

Her concern touched him. He closed his eyes and tilted his head to catch the light rain on his face. "It's actually quite refreshing."

Kara shook her head. "Did he tell you what he wanted from me?"

Noah rolled his eyes. "That would involve him giving me a straight answer, I'm afraid."

Kara shrugged. "Well, I really need to be getting back to work."

Noah placed a hand on her arm. "Will you please let me know if he tries to set up another meeting?"

Kara kissed Abe on the cheek, and gave Abe the umbrella. She stepped under the bakery's awning. "I'll pick it up later." She cast Noah a fleeting glance before she opened the door. "I'll make sure someone calls the bookstore if he shows up again. Have a good day, gentlemen."

Chapter Eleven

Kara spoke to Ada early that morning before Joni woke up. Fred wasn't in any condition to attend graduation ceremonies. The twins would go over to their house to set up the equipment so he could watch Joni receive her diploma. She wiped away tears that hadn't stopped falling since their conversation. *Why do things like this happen to good people?* Fred had been looking forward to this day as if Joni were his own granddaughter.

At times like this, Kara wished she had a relationship with her parents. Not for her sake, but for Joni's. They had turned away from her the day she married Steven, telling her that she was dead to them that day. In reality, they didn't even know about Joni.

When Joni asked about her grandparents, Kara told her the truth. Even at the tender age of fourteen she hadn't felt sorry for herself. She'd wrapped her arms around Kara and told her it didn't matter because they had each other.

Her heart swelled with pride as she leaned against the doorframe of her daughter's bedroom. Her long amber curls fanned the pillow under her head. There truly were no words to describe a mother's love for her child. Joni's long lashes fluttered to reveal crystal blue eyes. Once she saw her mother, concern etched her flawless forehead.

"Mom? Is everything okay?"

Kara swiped at a fresh batch of tears rolling down her face. "I was just thinking how proud I am of you."

"Oh, Mom." Joni tossed the covers aside and threw her legs over the side of the bed."Are you going to be like this all day?" She stretched.

"Probably." Kara tittered. She could count on one hand the number of times she'd cried in front of her daughter.

Joni rolled her eyes. "Remind me not to look at you when I'm giving my speech."

"I don't know why I'm so emotional." She shook her head. "It's a good thing the bakery is closed today."

She shrugged. "Probably hormones."

Kara choked. "What did you just say?"

"Well, you aren't getting any younger you know." Joni laughed and reached down to position her slippers.

Kara seized the opportunity and lunged on top of her, pinning her arms at her sides with her knees while she tickled her sensitive sides.

"Oh, my God! Stop!" Joni shrieked.

"Take it back!" Kara continued to tickle despite her pleas for her to stop. "Take it back!"

Joni gasped for breath. "Okay, okay...I take it back."

Mother and daughter collapsed onto their backs, panting to catch their breath.

Kara stared up at the ceiling and heard Joni let out a rush of air. These were the moments she must imbed into her memory for when she was away at college.

"Mom, what's going to happen to the bakery when school starts in the fall?"

"I don't know, honey. Today your only concern is to look beautiful and have a wonderful graduation. We'll figure something out."

Joni curled up against her side. "If you need me to stay, I will."

Kara swallowed hard. Joni would give up her college dream if she thought her mom needed her. Never had she heard such a selfless offer. "If I have any hope of keeping it together today, you've got to stop saying things like that." She sniffed.

"Okay. I don't know about you, but I'm starved."

Kara scrambled from the bed. "Last one to the kitchen makes breakfast."

Joni shrieked and bolted past her down the stairs. "And does the dishes!"

Noah noted the sign on the bakery door: CLOSED and Happy

Graduation to Joni and the twins. He wondered if it would be out of line to send flowers to the house. From what he'd seen, Joni was a good kid. He envied the relationship the mother and daughter shared. How he wished his mother could have given him that kind of love. He shook his head, refusing to let his mind wander in that direction. His mother did the best she could, and it was just plain selfish to have expected any more than that from her.

His father was another story. He'd agreed to give him a few moments of his time before lunch. No way was he going to interrupt Joni's special day with business.

Abe stopped sweeping the sidewalk out front of the bookstore. "Good morning, Noah. How are things at home this morning?"

Noah shrugged. "Same as always. No change unfortunately."

"Maybe tomorrow." Abe pat his back. "You mustn't give up hope."

"It's strange seeing the bakery closed, isn't it?"

"It's the first time in all the years I've been here." He clicked his tongue. "I didn't think anything would keep Fred away. Maybe there's more going on than meets the eye."

The same thoughts had crossed his mind, but he convinced himself he was over-reacting. "Why do you say that?"

"Fred hasn't been at the bakery for almost a week or better. Ada's not there either. Kara and those three kids are running the show."

"I hope the old-timer's okay."

His grandfather shook his head and opened the door to the bookstore. "Unfortunately we all got to go sometime."

Could it be? Was Fred sick? He'd better keep this bit of info from his father or he'd have the vultures circling.

"Do you think it's out of line for me to send Joni flowers for her graduation?"

Abe smiled a knowing smile. "Sign the card from both of us; she's a good kid."

"You don't think Kara will think it's a ploy to try and get in her good graces?"

Abe stopped and turned to face him. "Is it?"

Noah frowned. "Of course not."

"Than send the flowers. You worry too much." He waved him off and disappeared inside his office.

I have plenty to worry about. Noah wanted to talk to his grandfather about what his father had ordered him to do, but he didn't want to get him riled up again. He'd opened the bookstore to separate himself from all of the Steele bullshit.

"I'll be right back. I'm going to the flower shop."

"Good, and don't forget to sign the card from me too."

Chapter Twelve

An intoxicating wave of floral splendour wafted into her bedroom. A burst of red and yellow preceded her daughter's appearance in the doorway. "Oh my, aren't they beautiful." Kara had a feeling Fred and Ada would send her flowers.

"They really are." Joni nuzzled the bouquet, inhaling deeply. "I must say, I'm a little surprised."

Kara ran a brush through her hair. "Why would you be surprised? It's no secret how much you mean to them."

"It's been a secret to me. I've never even met Abe before, and I've only seen Noah that one time."

Kara stopped in mid-stroke. "Noah and Abe? From the bookstore?"

Joni shrugged and set the vase down on her dressing table. "It's a nice gesture though, isn't it?"

Kara smiled. "We better get dressed. The twins will be here in less than half an hour. Tyler just called and said they were leaving Fred and Ada's to get dressed."

"I can't wait for you to see my dress."

"I can't believe you've kept it a secret for this long."

Joni giggled, her eyes sparkling. "Me neither!" She spun on her heel and left the room.

Kara lay her brush down and cupped one of the delicate blooms. Maybe she should've invited him. The thought had crossed her mind. She'd decided against it given the emotional state she'd been in the past few days. The last thing she wanted was for Noah to see her with red eyes and a puffy nose. *No, my daughter deserves my full attention on her special day.*

She'd actually bought a new dress for the occasion. Shopping for one had been an experience in itself. Luckily, the sales clerk knew what she was doing and helped her pick out one that complimented her body. The silky emerald green dress slid down her long body, settling perfectly over her curves. The sales clerk asked her how it felt, not if she liked it or not. The dress made her feel very special, and the woman looking back at her in the mirror brought a smile to her face. She'd chosen to wear her hair down, simply because she loved the way it looked against the dress. Bronze metallic strappy shoes completed her look.

"Mom, can you give me a hand?"

Kara knew her daughter would be stunning in whatever dress she chose, but nothing could have prepared her for the vision of loveliness in front of the full length mirror.

"Will you zip me?"

Rendered speechless, Kara zipped Joni's floor-length gown. The material was the same texture as hers, but the color...never had she seen a more beautiful shade of purple. Joni faced her, and Kara fanned her face to keep the tears at bay. The elegant sweetheart neckline against her porcelain skin took her breath away.

"Don't start already." Joni's bottom lip trembled, and she focused on trying to tame a stray ringlet.

Kara opened her eyes as wide as possible and smiled.

"I take it you approve?" She fluttered her eyelashes—a vision of pure loveliness.

Kara pressed her lips firmly together. "Mmhm."

A knock on the door pulled Kara from her trance-like state. Joni drifted past her to answer the door. Kara stood in place, attempting to regain some semblance of composure. Her daughter's delighted shrieks brought her to the stairs. "What's going on?"

Joni stood next to the two very handsome twins, pointing outside at a limo parked out front.

"How cool is that? That was very nice of you two."

"I wish we could take the credit, but Fred and Ada are the ones who made the arrangements."

Kara exchanged a look with her daughter, blinking away the tears.

"Can we stop to see them before we go to grad?" Joni

pleaded.

"I've got a better idea." Kara took her by the hand and led her into the living room. "Is everything set up?"

"Just give me a couple of seconds." Tyler went over to the shelf beside the television and turned on the equipment he'd brought over earlier that day when Joni was out getting her hair done.

Joni's brow creased. "What's all this?"

"Ready?" asked Tyler.

"Watch and see." Kara gave Tyler a nod.

Tyler turned the television on. On the screen, Ada sat next to her husband on an oversized armchair. Other than the blanket draped across his lap and looking a little tired, one would never guess how sick Fred really was.

Joni's hands flew to her cheeks and her eyes brimmed. "Fred...Ada?"

The couple smiled. Ada dabbed at her eyes with a crumpled hanky.

"Joni, I don't think I've seen anything more beautiful than the way you look tonight." Fred said hoarsely.

"Thank you." She replied, barely above a whisper.

"I'm sorry I had to get sick and miss your graduation." His voice cracked, and Ada stroked his weathered hand.

"We want you to know that we couldn't be more proud of you if you were our own granddaughter." Ada dabbed at her eyes once again. "I gave that young man a gift to give you."

Tyson handed a stunned Joni, a long velvet jewellery box.

"Go ahead, open it." Ada waved her on.

Joni's bewildered gaze travelled to Kara.

"Go on." Kara prompted.

Her hands trembled as she opened the box. Inside, an exquisite diamond teardrop necklace rested on a velvet lining. Joni gasped as she searched the old woman's face on the TV screen.

"My mother gave it to me when I graduated." Her voice cracked and tears rolled freely down her flushed cheeks. "It would mean so much to me if you'd accept it."

"I...I don't know what to say..."

Kara took the necklace from her trembling hands and helped to put it on. The diamond sparkled, lying perfectly at the hollow of her neck.

"I've never owned anything like this before." She sniffled.

"One day you will pass it on to your daughter on her graduation day." Ada beamed.

"I love it." Her fingers traced the pendant gently, as if it would shatter if she pressed too hard. "I love you both. Thank you."

Fred nudged his wife. "What about the envelope?"

"Oh." Tyler reached inside his jacket and pulled out a long envelope that he handed to Joni.

Tears spilled down her face as she opened it. Her hands shook, and her jaw dropped as she passed Kara the paper.

"Paid in full." She scanned the letter's contents. "Tuition, books, and room for the next four years of college." Kara could hardly believe what she was looking at.

Joni dissolved into her mother's arms. Tyler and Tyson exchanged an uncomfortable look and averted their gazes.

Fred laid his hand on his wife's lap, and she clasped it. Both of their eyes glistened with unshed tears. "We want you to go to college and not have to worry about a thing."

"I'm speechless." She shuddered.

"You don't have to say anything. Have a wonderful evening, and when the time comes to go to college, knock 'em dead." Fred winked. "Now enough of this mushy stuff, you have a speech to give, don't you?" He sank back in the chair, his pallor considerably whiter than when they had turned the TV on. "This old man needs to take a wee nap before then."

"I am so going to hug your neck the next time I see you." Joni sniffled.

"And I am so going to let you." His voice cracked.

Ada reached for the controller. "We'll check back in with you all in a bit."

The evening couldn't have gone any better if it had been orchestrated. Joni gave her speech and had half of her classmates in tears. Unexpectedly, she also won the Award of Excellence for top honours in all of her seven business courses. By the time the graduation ceremonies were over, Kara was emotionally spent.

"The limo can take you home and then come back to wait for the dance to end." Joni gave her mother the award and her diploma. "Did Fred and Ada see everything okay?"

"Yes, I called them to make sure. I'm so glad they were able to watch you graduate."

"Me too." Her hand went to her necklace. "I still can't believe everything they've done for me."

"You mean the world to them. Now go and have fun. My bed is calling me."

Joni laughed. She threw her arms around her neck, knocking her back a couple of steps.

"Easy now. You don't want the old girl to break a hip, do you?"

"Oh, Mom."

Once Kara said her goodbyes, she allowed the chauffer to help her into the back of the limo. Her fingers travelled over the plush fabric of the seat. *So this is how the other half lives.* Her thoughts drifted to Noah Steele. *He was probably driven back and forth to school in one of these*. Sadness enveloped her.

Even on the night of her daughter's graduation, Noah managed to find a way into her thoughts. His world was so cold and polished. Had he ever experienced the kind of bond she shared with Joni? She'd met Caleb, and heard more than enough about his father. *What about Noah's mother?*

At home, she saw the light flash next to the phone and stabbed the message button.

"Kara? It's Ada, please, I need you...oh God, please don't let it be too late."

Chapter Thirteen

"Have you learned nothing from me?" Zachary Steele leaned back in his chair and narrowed his eyes on his eldest son. "There's something more going on at that bakery. It has never been closed for two days in a row."

"Just what exactly are you saying, Father?" Noah wasn't crazy about the direction of their conversation.

"I'm saying, when opportunity presents itself, one must grab hold of it."

"I don't think now is the time to coerce Ms. Walker into leaving the bakery." *Could you be more insensitive?*

"I agree. I think now is the time to make an offer for the entire bakery."

"You must be joking. I will not do any such thing. Whatever has closed the bakery must be pretty serious."

"I don't have time to argue with you. Either you do this, or I'll find someone who will."

I'm a fool to have hung on to the hope there was still a heart behind his father's Steele walls. Noah struggled to contain his anger. "Can I at least find out why they've closed the bakery? Word has it, Fred, the owner, hasn't been well."

"Exactly why we need to act now. Maybe his wife will be relieved not to have the stress of running the business."

Noah expelled a long breath. "Give me one week."

His father huffed. "You have three days, no more. I've already wasted enough time pussyfooting around because of you."

If it wasn't for the promise he'd made to his mother four years ago, he would have stood up right then and there and told his father to go to Hell. How was it possible he had the same blood as this cold, callous man running through his veins?

Zachary Steele jotted down a few notes in the leather journal that sat on the desk. "You know, if I asked your brother to do this for me, he'd have already done so with no questions asked." He shook his head in disgust.

Rather than respond and risk losing his temper, Noah stood.

"If that's everything, I better get moving."

"Make them an offer they can't refuse." Zachary said without looking up.

Noah left his father's office, a myriad of emotions battling inside of him. How he wanted to pack his things and leave this hell once and for all.

A new sign hung on the bakery's door that morning: Closed Until Further Notice. His gut told him something bad was going on, and if his hunch was correct, Fred had taken a turn for the worse.

I better find some answers fast.

Blinded by a veil of tears, Kara stumbled up the front steps at Fred and Ada's house. Her heel caught on the hem of her dress and she fell to her knees. Her pain-filled cry resounded in the night as the concrete shredded her dress and grazed her knees.

"Damn!"

Strong hands helped her to her feet.

"Are you okay?" asked a middle-aged man toting a doctor's bag.

The front door flew open, and Ada grabbed hold of the startled man's arm and pulled him inside.

"Hurry! Please, you must hurry!" Ada sobbed. She led the doctor into the bedroom and closed the door behind them.

Kara followed them into the house. She stood with her back against the wall. Slowly, she slid down it until she sat on the wood floor, her battered knees drawn to her chest. She stared at the closed bedroom door for what seemed like an eternity, praying the doctor had gotten there in time to help Fred.

Her breathing labored upon seeing the doorknob turn. Ada emerged with red-rimmed eyes and leaned heavily against the doctor.

"How is he?" she asked, terrified of the answer.

Ada sighed wearily.

"He's resting comfortably for now." The doctor patted Ada's hand reassuringly.

"Does he need to go to the hospital?"

He shook his head solemnly. "There's nothing there we can't do for him here. Besides, he's quite adamant about staying home.

"What can I do to help?" Kara stood up.

"All we can do is keep him as comfortable as possible."

Kara blinked back the tears. "How much longer does he have?" She choked on the sour bile rising up the back of her throat.

"I have no way of knowing." He led Ada to the sofa and helped her to sit down. "It could be a couple of weeks...or as little as a couple of hours."

"Is he awake?"

"He slips in and out. He's been asking for you."

"You go to him." Ada spoke barely above a whisper. "I'd like a word with the doctor."

Cold tendrils of fear gripped Kara's heart as she braced herself to enter the bedroom. She took a deep breath and inched the door open. Fred lay on the bed, a shadow of the man who had greeted her each morning with a smile. The white sheet that covered his body rose slightly with each shallow breath he took. His eyes remained closed as she reached his bedside. Gently, she covered his pale hand with hers. His eyes fluttered open, and he struggled to focus.

"Kara," he said breathlessly.

"Hush, you need your strength." *Please.....oh God, please don't take him now.*

"The bakery...." His chest heaved as he tried to talk.

"I'll take care of the bakery. You need to stay calm and save your energy." Tears fell from her eyes, dampening the white sheet.

"I want...I want you to have it."

"I don't understand."

"Ada will help you. Promise me you'll keep the bakery open." He winced and grabbed his chest.

"Please, Fred, you must try not to talk."

"I don't have much time." He squeezed her hand. "The bakery

is yours. Promise me you'll keep it open."

"Fred," Kara sobbed.

"Please, Kara...*promise* me."

"Yes, Fred. I promise. Please, you need to calm down."

His body relaxed the instant she promised. His lips parted. "Ada."

Kara blindly ran from the room to find Ada taking the medicine from the doctor to keep Fred comfortable.

"He wants you." She didn't....she *couldn't* put up a brave front.

Ada pushed the bottles of pills back in the doctor's hands and ran to the bedroom, closing the door behind her.

An incessant knock sounded on the front door. Kara trudged over to answer it. She opened the door, and Joni crumpled into her arms. Kara led her daughter to the couch where they sat wrapped in each other's arms, sobbing.

"Why is this happening, Mom? He was fine last night."

Kara wished she had some magic words to take the pain from her daughter. "He's been sick a lot longer than any of us knew, Joni."

Silence permeated the small home as the bedroom door opened. Ada walked out, looking lost and disorientated. Without having to say a word, they all knew Fred had passed away. Ada joined them on the couch where they sat huddled.

Ada broke the silence. "He made me promise to help you keep the bakery open. It's yours now. I will help any way I can."

"I'll keep my promise, Ada. The bakery will re-open when the time is right."

Chapter Fourteen

Noah shivered and buttoned the top two buttons of his coat. An ominous gray sky, coupled with a brisk morning breeze blowing off of the St. Lawrence, held the threat of rain. Grief shrouded Main Street—handwritten signs hung in many of the storefront windows he passed, explaining their locked doors. Fred Meyers had touched so many lives in some way. It was only fitting they'd want to say their final goodbyes on the day he was laid to rest.

The shrill ring of his cell phone jarred him from his thoughts just as he reached the bookstore. "Hello?"

"Noah? Have you forgotten you were supposed to call me this morning with an update? I trust you have good news for me."

He glanced at his watch, noting the early hour of his father's call. "I'm afraid I have only bad news this morning, Father. Fred Meyers passed away. In fact, I'm picking up Gramps right now, and we're headed to the funeral."

"Perfect. I'm sure you'll find an opportunity to take Ms. Walker aside to discuss our offer."

"You're kidding, right?" He shook his head. *How is it possible I have the same blood running through my veins?*

"Now, Noah, there's no room for sentiment in business matters."

Noah counted to ten under his breath. *There's no way in hell I'm going to talk to Kara about this on today of all days.* "Listen, I can't talk about this right now. If you've one ounce of compassion in you, you'll back off. I'll come over and discuss this after the service today." He gritted his teeth, waiting for his response.

"I'll expect to see you this afternoon. Don't make me wait all day."

He put a hand over the phone while he let out the breath he'd been holding. "Of course, Father."

The line went dead.

The front door to the bookstore opened, and Abe stepped out, concern lined his weathered face. "Let me guess? Your father?"

Noah shook his head. "He sure is a piece of work."

"What's he done this time?" Abe slipped on a pair of leather gloves.

"That man has about as much compassion as a rock. Can you believe he actually wanted me to make an offer on the bakery today?" Noah shook his head.

"I hope you told him where to stuff that offer."

His grandfather's cheeks coloured, and Noah regretted telling him anything. "I told him I'd stop by later this afternoon to discuss it."

"You mean *we* will pay him a visit."

Noah squeezed his grandfather's shoulder. "I can handle him on my own. Thanks anyways."

"I wasn't asking permission, Noah. We'll head to the estate after the service." He dipped his head, signalling they continue on their way. "We better get a move on or we'll be late for the service."

They walked to the car in silence. One thing Noah knew for certain: once his grandfather made up his mind about something, not much could sway him. He made a concerted effort to push all thoughts of his father to the back of his mind as he drove to the small church on the edge of the city, by the river. The packed parking lot explained the absence of traffic on the way there.

"Do you want me to let you off at the door while I park?"

Abe frowned. "I'm not an invalid. I can walk, you know."

They had to park on the street and walk up the lane to the church. Inside, they were ushered to a seat near the back. He spotted Kara in the front row with Ada between her and Joni. The three women held on to each other through the entire service. An abundance of flowers cascaded from the altar. Every person who'd ever been a customer at the bakery had come to pay their respects. Noah and Abe sat in silence.

The crowd rose as the twins led the procession from the church. Kara and Joni walked on either side of a very distraught widow, practically carrying her down the aisle. Neither Joni nor Kara's attention strayed from their charge, their faces pale and etched in pain. Noah physically ached to comfort this woman who'd taken up residence in his heart.

They followed the stream of mourners from the church to the hall. Abe made a beeline for the table set up with sandwiches and Kara's desserts. Noah scanned the room until he spotted Kara at the opposite end of the hall. She sat with Ada and Joni, nodding politely as mourners offered their condolences. A group of people blocked his view just as he heard a familiar voice. He spun around to find Caleb standing next to his grandfather.

What the hell is he doing here? He clenched his fists. *Not on my watch, little brother.* He glared at Caleb until he finally took notice of him. Their gazes locked, and he stopped talking in mid-sentence. His grandfather stepped between them just as Noah broke through the crowd.

"What the hell are you doing here?" Noah asked as forcefully as he could without drawing attention.

"Why, I'm here for the same reasons as you are." He straightened his tie. "To offer my condolences."

"I highly doubt that, little brother." Noah seethed. "You stay the hell away from Kara and Ada."

"Okay boys." Abe put a hand on each of their chests. "Now is not the time for this sibling rivalry."

"I couldn't agree more...which is why you were just about to leave."He stared intently into Caleb's eyes.

Caleb shook his head. "I don't know why you think you have the right to tell me what I can and cannot do. I'll leave as soon as I have a moment with Ms. Walker."

Noah reached past Abe and grabbed hold of Caleb's arm, squeezing with all his strength. Pain flashed in his brothers' eyes, and he tried to pull away.

"You will either leave on your own accord, or I will throw your scrawny ass out of here."

"You wouldn't want to upset poor Ada by creating a scene, would you?"

"Don't underestimate me. I've wanted to kick your ass for some time now."

"Okay, okay. Nobody's going to kick anyone's ass—at least not here. We'll all leave together." Abe raised a wrinkled hand. "Now!"

Noah pressed his lips firmly together. He followed the two of them out, purposely avoiding the curious looks from a certain someone at the other end of the hall.

"Both of you get in the car." Abe stormed over to Noah's car and opened both passenger doors. "Get in! I'm driving."

"You can't tell me what to do, old man." Caleb folded his arms across his chest.

"Do you want to bet on that?" Abe raised his cane in the air.

Caleb put out his hands in defence. "Just where do you think you're taking us?"

Anger flashed in his grandfather's eyes. "I'm putting an end to all of this bull today."

"What bull?" asked Caleb.

"How about the little matter of your father wanting to buy the bakery? Or that he actually expected one of you to make an offer today of all days? Now are you going to get in or do I have to help you?"

Laughter danced in his eyes. "Okay, but I'll drive over there myself. I'm not leaving my car here." The corner of his mouth curled in a devilish smile.

Abe jabbed a finger at his youngest grandson's chest. "You better be there or..." He waved a hand in disgust and rounded the front of the car to sit behind the wheel.

Noah watched his brother strut over to his car. It took every ounce of restraint not to wipe the self-satisfied smirk off of his face.

It worried him to see his grandfather so angry. A sheen of perspiration covered his flushed face. "Are you okay, Gramps?"

"I will be after I have a talk with that son of mine." He

grimaced. "I've sat back long enough and watched him mistreat people to get what he wants." The smack of his hand against the steering wheel reverberated within the car. "Not anymore!"

"Okay. I can see you're determined to do this, but you need to calm down a bit. You're face is as red as a tomato."

Abe focused on the road ahead of him. A symphony of emotions played across his reddened face. Noah needed to calm him down some before he faced his father. "Why don't we stop and grab a coffee? We can plan our strategy, and you'll set my mind at ease by cooling off a little."

Abe sighed, signalling as he turned into a gas bar with a diner behind it. "You need gas anyway."

Kara caught a glimpse of the three Steele men leaving the hall. *How nice of them to show their respects. Maybe I have the Steele men pegged wrong.*

"If you don't mind, I'm rather tired." Ada whispered in her ear. "Do you think it would be okay if I go home?"

"Of course it's okay. It's been a long week for all of us." Kara tapped Joni on the shoulder. "Would you gather up our things and let the twins know it's time to take Ada home?"

"Sure." She kissed Ada's cheek. "I'll be right back."

Ada never looked so tired, or as old. Not that she could even begin to imagine how she must be feeling. She'd been married to Fred for almost fifty years. For the first time, she understood when people said losing a spouse was like losing a physical part of them. The death of Joni's father hadn't affected her as intensely. Perhaps it would have if theirs had been a happy marriage.

Within minutes, the twins were at Ada's side to escort her through the crowd. Kara followed with Joni firmly latched to her arm. They hardly spoke a word on the drive back to Ada's house. Ada sat with her head resting on Kara's arm. From time to time, a shudder ran through her frail body.

Once inside, Kara settled Ada on the couch, and Joni put the kettle on for tea. The twins busied themselves dismantling the camera they'd set up for Joni's graduation.

"There's really no need for you all to be fussing over me like this. I don't want your own lives to stop because of me."

"I wouldn't want to be anywhere else right now, Ada." Kara smiled.

Her thin lips quivered, and her hands dropped to her sides. "I don't know what I'm supposed to do now." Tears flowed freely down her flushed cheeks.

"Oh, Ada. For now, you don't need to do anything."

She slowly closed her eyes. "I don't think I've ever been so tired."

"Why don't you go lie down for a while?"

Kara helped her up from the couch and led her to the bedroom. Both stopped in the doorway, their gazes settled on the crumpled bed where Fred had passed.

"I can't." Ada leaned heavily against her.

"If you want, I can strip the bed and remake it with clean sheets."

Ada shook her head vigorously and made her way to the bed. Her fingers feathered the indent in the pillow where Abe's head had lain.

Kara wasn't comfortable watching such an intimate moment, but she didn't want to leave her friend alone.

Ada gathered the pillow to her chest and buried her face in it. She drew in a shaky before unleashing a fresh torrent of tears.

The kettle whistled, and Kara tore herself from the room. Maybe she did need some time alone to grieve after all.

Kara took teacups from the cupboard, and Joni answered a knock on the door. She looked fixedly at Caleb Steele.

What the hell's he doing here? Something's going on, and it has nothing to do with him offering condolences. She stepped in front of her daughter. "Now's really not a good time, Mr. Steele. Ada's retired to her room for the evening."

She nudged Joni back, and Caleb stepped forward, reaching past her to give Joni a flower arrangement.

"Please offer Mrs. Meyers my deepest sympathy."

Sympathy, my ass.

"Why don't we talk outside?" she said through clenched teeth.

He seemed a little rattled. *Maybe he wasn't expecting me to be here.* She leaned against the railing and folded her arms across her chest.

"How about we stop playing games, Mr. Steele? You've obviously had something on your mind for some time now. You have my full attention."

Caleb straightened his stance. "I want you to know, on behalf of my family, how deeply sorry we are to hear of Fred's passing."

Kara felt her composure slipping. She raised a hand to stop his line of bullshit. "Cut the crap. You've been stalking me for days now. We both know this has nothing to do with your concern for Fred's wife, or, for that matter, any of us. Why don't you stop insulting my intelligence and tell me the real reason you've come here?"

He fidgeted with his tie. "You made quite the impression with your desserts at Steele Towers." He clasped his hands. "My father's very pleased with all the praise he's received since he came home from abroad." He smiled a practiced smile. "So much so, he initially wanted to offer you a position in our kitchens."

Kara's eyes widened in surprise. "I'm quite happy at the bakery, Mr. Steele. I have no desire to leave."

He nodded. "I had a feeling you'd say that."

"So we understand each other. I best be getting back inside." Kara pushed off the railing.

"Please, this will only take a minute."

She folded her arms across her chest, her patience growing thinner.

"I think I have a proposition where everybody wins."

"Get to the point, Mr. Steele."

"Steele Enterprises would like to make an offer on the bakery, and we'd like you to continue being a part of it."

Kara could hardly process the words coming out of his mouth. This man had the audacity to come here on the day they'd put Fred to rest and make an offer on the bakery. She wrestled with an overwhelming urge to blacken both of his eyes.

"I want you to listen closely. I'm only going to say this once." She clenched her fists. "How dare you come here the day of Fred's funeral, under the pretence you actually give a shit."

"Now Kara, that's not true. I'll—"

She straightened her stance and jabbed a finger at his chest. "Don't patronize me. Fred had one dying wish...." Her voice cracked. "To keep the bakery open and that's exactly what I intend to do." She stormed over to the door and spun around to face him. "The bakery's not for sale. In fact, as of today, we'll no longer be doing business with you or any other Steele for that matter." She swiped at the tears rolling down her face. "I don't want to see your face again. Do I make myself clear?"

Caleb's face turned beet red. "Perhaps you need some time to think on this."

Kara let out a cry of frustration. "Go away or I'll call the police. You're not welcome here." She slammed the door behind her and leaned against the wall, gasping for breath. *Thank God it wasn't Ada who answered the door.*

Caleb hadn't been at the funeral to show his respect for Fred. He was there on business. Did Abe catch on to his ruse? Is that why they left the funeral together? How was it possible Abe and Noah were related to Caleb and Zachary? If she were smart, she'd wash her hands of the whole Steele mess. She slipped unnoticed into the bathroom to wash away any traces of her upset.

Chapter Fifteen

Noah closed the heavy wooden door as quietly as possible. *Phew! I can't believe it worked.* He convinced Abe to visit with Glenda first. Luckily she reacted as he had hoped and his grandfather agreed to have tea with his mother. Judging by his expression when Noah excused himself, he wasn't pulling anything over on the old man.

Mother was so pleased to have a gentleman caller; she'd be very upset if he left before tea was served. Sadly, she didn't know who Abe was, but she was very happy to have the company. Gramps didn't have it him to intentionally upset someone, especially his daughter-in-law who he hadn't seen in over a year.

The sudden rush of air warned of someone's approach mere seconds before his red-faced brother sped past him.

"Where's the fire?" asked Noah.

Caleb came to an abrupt stop. His eye twitched as it always did when angered. "That woman is a fool!"

"Keep the noise down. What woman has you all fired up?"

"Kara Walker, that's who. You wouldn't believe the way she just talked to me."

Noah pinned him to the wall without a second thought. "What the hell did you do now?"

"Get your hands off of me."

Spittle sprayed in Noah's face, intensifying his anger. "Not until you start talking."

Zachary Steele came out of his office and stormed toward them. "What the hell is going on out here?" He pried Noah from Caleb. "Both of you, in my office—now."

Noah glared at first his father then Caleb, who was massaging his arms where he grabbed him.

"Now!" Zachary barked.

Noah followed his father into the office. He'd never been so angry. *What the hell did he do to Kara?*

Zachary sat down behind his desk. "Now which one of you is going to tell me what that was all about?"

"Caleb was just about to tell me." Noah seethed.

"Caleb?"

"I just did what you wanted. I went to Kara Walker and offered to buy the bakery and her services."

"You son of a...." Noah gripped the arms of his chair. "For God's sake, Fred's body isn't even cold yet."

Zachary steepled his fingers under his chin. "And what did Ms. Walker say?"

"She turned me down flat, and she's refused to do business with any of us ever again."

"What do you mean by, *any* of us?" Noah grit his teeth.

"I think her exact words were: 'we will no longer be doing business with you or any other Steele.'"

"Just who in the hell do you think you are? I told you I'd take care of talking to her."

"And just when did you plan on doing so?" Caleb looked down his nose at him.

"That's enough. What's done is done. Obviously I should have handled things myself from the start."

All Noah could think about was Kara and what went through her mind when Caleb showed up. *Does she think I had anything to do with it?* He imagined how hurt she must feel, especially on today of all days. "This is total bullshit." Noah shook his head at both men before getting up and leaving the room.

"How dare you! Get back here this instant!" His father ran into the hallway after him, closely followed by Caleb.

Noah froze in place, and slowly turned to face him. "How dare I? You own half the town; what is so important about the bakery? Is it because you can't have it that makes you want it so badly?"

Zachary pursed his lips like he did when his patience grew thin. "I'm getting pretty tired of your attitude."

A door opened behind Noah, and he knew who it was before

he spoke.

"What the hell is going on out here?" He glowered at his son. "All of this yelling has upset *your wife.* You do remember you have a wife, don't you?"

"I suggest you change your tone with me, *Father.*" His venomous words spewed. "I don't have time to deal with the likes of you."

Zachary dismissed him with a drop of his chin, before shifting his verbal assault to Noah. "If you are so unhappy, why don't you leave? In fact, why don't you both leave...now!"

"How can you be so cruel?" Abe lowered his head. "I'm ashamed you have my blood running through those cold veins of yours."

"Save your pity party for your *bookstore.*" Caleb piped in from behind Zachary.

Noah took his shaking hand in his. "*Please* Gramps...go see if you can calm my mother."

Abe nodded sullenly, and without another word retreated.

The pain in his grandfather's voice refueled his anger, and he glared at his father.

"Shame on you...as for leaving, you know why I can't go." His father's suggestion, and the way he talked to Abe shouldn't have come as a surprise to him, but it did.

"It's not like you don't have any options," Caleb piped in. "I'm sure *Gramps* will take you in."

Noah threw up his hands. "I can't believe I'm related to either one of you. I promise you both; I will do everything in my power to see you don't get your filthy hands on that bakery."

"Careful, Noah..." Zachary leaned forward to stare directly into his eyes. "Don't put me in a position where I *make* you leave this estate."

Noah tilted his head back and laughed. "I think it's *you* who should be careful. You don't want word to get out about what kind of man you really are, do you?

His father slammed his fist against the wall. "I will not be talked to like this in my own home."

Noah matched his father's steely gaze. Every fiber of his being wanted to continue this fight, but he'd learned over the years when to walk away. Without another word, he slipped into the one place he knew they wouldn't follow, and closed the heavy wooden door securely behind him.

Kara sat with the twins and Joni while Ada slept. She told them all about Caleb's visit and his offer to buy the bakery.

"Needless to say, I told him where he could stick his offer. I'm going to need all your help to re-open the bakery. I made a promise to Fred to keep it open and I fully intend on keeping it."

"Why don't we all meet at the store tomorrow and get things started?" Tyson held on to Joni's hand as he spoke.

"You boys have been a godsend." Kara smiled warmly at the twins. "It's going to be tough replacing the three of you when school starts in the fall."

Joni opened her mouth to speak.

"No, postponing school is not an option." She wagged her finger at her daughter.

Ada walked into the room, rubbing her eyes. "Who wants to postpone school?"

"No one. Right, Joni?"

Joni laughed. "Right, Mom." She rolled her eyes and stood. "Why don't I heat up a couple of casseroles?"

"That sounds like a great idea." Kara joined Ada and helped her over to the sofa. "You haven't eaten today, have you?"

Ada shrugged. "I don't remember." She sat in the corner of the sofa, looking lost and disorientated.

Kara took a knitted throw from the end of the couch and laid it across her lap. She wished there was something she could do to put a smile on her dear friend's face, but she knew it was simply too soon. The twins joined Joni in the kitchen where she enlisted their help to do up the dishes and set the table. Ada wasn't the only one physically and emotionally drained. Kara stifled a yawn and sat next to Ada.

"Is there anything I can get for you?" She smoothed down her dishevelled hair.

Ada shook her head, her eyes filling with moisture again. "How am I going to go on without him? Did you know I have never been apart from him...not even for a day, in over fifty years?"

Kara swallowed hard. "I wish I had answers for you. All we can do for now, is keep our promise and re-open the bakery. You're not alone, Ada. You have four people in this house who love you very much."

Ada leaned her head on Kara's shoulder and sighed.

"Dinner is served." Joni set a steaming casserole on a hotplate in the center of the table.

They ate meagre helpings of a beef casserole in silence. Ada managed to eat only a few spoonfuls of supper before she excused herself and retreated to the bedroom she'd shared with Fred. Joni convinced Kara to go home and get some rest by agreeing to spend the night there with Ada. Reluctantly, she let Tyler drive her back to the apartment.

"Be sure to call me if Ada needs me." Kara stepped out of the truck, mindful of a puddle at the curb.

Inside, the light flashed on the answering machine and she noted twenty messages of which she had no desire to hear. She moved robotically up the stairs to the bathroom and started the bath. She just needed to turn all the turmoil off, if even for a short time while she soaked in the tub.

The scent of roses filled the hallway. The gorgeous bouquet from Abe and Noah sat where she'd left them on her dressing table. Angry tears prickled the backs of her eyelids. She closed her eyes and pictured the three Steele men leaving the hall after the funeral.

Noah had to have known of his father's offer for the bakery. After all, he lived in the glitzy Steele Estate. If it was true that he didn't want to be judged because of his station in life, why did he still live there?

Was it all part of some elaborate scheme? Why the bakery? Is it just another piece of property to add to the Steele Monopoly board? It was all about power, and they didn't care who they stomped over to get what they wanted, including taking advantage of a grieving widow on the day of her husband's funeral. The same way they'd given her no option but to sell the farmhouse to pay off Steven's debt to Steele Enterprises.

Kara picked up the bouquet from the vase and threw them in the trash can. "They can all go to hell." She said firmly at her reflection in the mirror.

Chapter Sixteen

Kara woke to a wet, dreary morning befitting her foul mood. Despite how sickened she'd been with the whole Steele ordeal, her dreams were filled with Noah and how handsome he'd been that night on the boat.

Things would have ended very differently that night if they hadn't been interrupted. Thank God things didn't get that far. The ache in her heart was nothing compared to how she would have felt if she'd slept with him.

She'd woken once drenched in sweat, her body ached with longing as she remembered her dream. He'd lowered her to a lounge chair on the deck, a canopy of twinkling stars above as he rained sweet kisses.... Kara shook her head. While he made love to her in the moonlight; his brother was probably changing the locks on the bakery door.

The ringing phone pulled her thoughts back to the present. She fumbled with the phone on her bedside table. "Hello?"

"Mom? Is everything okay?"

"Joni? Yes, what time is it?" Relief and disappointed dueled within her. Relief it wasn't a Steele on the phone, and at the same time, disappointed it wasn't Noah.

"It's almost noon. I thought you were going to the bakery first thing this morning."

Kara slowly pushed herself up to lean against the headboard. She hadn't slept this late in years. "Oh, my God. I'm so sorry. Can you believe I'm still in bed?"

"Didn't you hear Tyler at the door?"

"The first thing I heard since going to bed last night was the phone ringing just now."

"You're not getting sick are you?"

Kara put a hand to her forehead. "No, I don't think so. It must be the lack of sleep this week."

"Why don't you let the twins handle the deliveries this afternoon?"

"No, that's okay, I'm getting up now." Kara lifted the covers off of her and slid to the side of the bed. "See if one of the twins will pick me up. I don't feel like taking the bus today."

"Tyson will be there in an hour. That gives you half an hour before the first delivery is due."

"Wonderful, I don't have to rush. How is Ada this morning?"

Joni sighed. "It's just so unfair, Mom. She looks so lost. I heard her up walking around a few times last night."

The tremor in her daughter's voice gave away how hard she was taking Fred's passing, despite the brave front she tried to pull off.

"Make sure you give her a big squeeze for me. I'll be there right after work."

"I'll stay with her until you get here. Tyson can help with the deliveries."

"Thanks honey. Even if Ada stays quiet today, you can bet she's glad she isn't alone."

"Okay, see you later. I'm going to start some laundry."

"See you..." Kara pulled the phone from her ear and jerked it back. "Joni?"

"Mom?"

"If any man carrying the Steele name comes by, shoot first and ask questions later."

Joni laughed. "Don't worry, none of those guys are getting anywhere near Ada."

"You're a chip off the old block."

"Is that a good thing?"

Kara stroked her jaw. "I haven't decided yet."

"Well, I have, and it's a very good thing. Now go get in the shower."

"Yes ma'am. I love you Joni."

"Back atcha, now git!" Her laughter faded as she set the phone on its cradle.

Kara swung her legs over the side of the bed and wiped the

sleep from her eyes. She stretched her arms out and fell backwards, staring up at the ceiling fan moving just enough to circulate the air.

Hopefully nobody from the bookstore notices she was she was at the bakery for deliveries. She wasn't in the mood for any further altercations with *any* of the Steele men. By now, they probably knew about her turning down Caleb. She doubted he'd told them exactly what was said. She nickered. Although the timing couldn't have been worse, she somewhat enjoyed putting the pompous ass in his place.

Abe and Noah would be another matter. She was emotionally vested in the two of them. It wouldn't be so easy if she was put in a position to tell them what they could do with their offers. She hoisted herself up, fuelled by pent-up anger, and stomped down the hall to the bathroom.

Noah's stomach churned. He felt physically ill after Caleb told him about his talk with Kara. Thankfully Abe never held a grudge for setting him up with Glenda. In fact, a sadness had come over him, so unlike his grandfather's usual optimistic self.

He sat on the sofa in the communal area of the west wing of the estate. He admired the two overstuffed wingback chairs in front of the fireplace. His mother did a terrific job of reupholstering them to match the rusty brown drapes. The entire room was done in earth tones, making it feel like fall no matter the time of year.

The rest of the estate was nothing like their wing. Not one room could be classed as warm and inviting. Even in the rooms with a fireplace, a chill in the air never seemed to go away. He stood and stretched before meandering to the kitchen. They didn't have a twenty-four chef like his father and Caleb did, opting to keep staff to a minimum.

A plate of cinnamon buns sat next to the percolator making its final gurgles. He picked up a sticky bun and accessed it. *Is this one of hers?* They were a regular customer, at least they *were* before yesterday happened. He set the bun back down and licked his fingers. *Maybe I'll visit Gramps and see if anyone is at the bakery.* He didn't want to talk to her about any of this so soon after Fred's death, but his father was pissed off, and when he was, he was relentless. Her delicacies and the bakery itself weren't even important to him right now. She was a property on the Steele Monopoly Board, and Zachary Steele wouldn't be happy until he owned it, and her.

Noah ran his fingers down the length of his hair. It felt good to have it down for a change. There must be some way to resolve this situation without losing her. He could just imagine what conclusions she'd already drawn where he was concerned.

The bed in the master bedroom creaked. Noah smiled and walked over to the piano. He wasn't a concert pianist by any means, but he wasn't an amateur either. He wiggled his fingers and sat on the bench. It had been quite some time since he played for her. Maybe if she woke to her favourite song, she'd have a good day. The sultry tones of Diana Krall's, *Gentle Rain*, floated upwards from the piano on the wings of a crescendo.

Although he played for her, when he closed his eyes, it was Kara he saw. They were aboard the boat, dancing in the moonlight. Her head rest against his chest as they glided around the perimeter. Her head tilted upwards, and he dipped to capture her full lips. Her heart pounded against his chest, and he deepened the kiss, tugging playfully at her bottom lip.

"Housekeeping."

The maid, Debra, ended his daydream. Startled, he took his fingers from the keys and quickly shifted to hide the heat rushing to his cheeks. *Blushing? At my age?*

"I'm sorry to interrupt, Noah." The tiny slip of a woman carried a stack of towels. "Please don't stop on my account. Is the missus awake?"

Noah got up from the piano. "I think she's just waking up now."

Debra smiled and ducked inside the bathroom. "Do you want me to come back later, Noah? You're usually gone by now."

"No, I'll just finish dressing and be out of your way."

"Fine. Are there any special instructions today?"

Noah shook his head and got up from the piano. "Not today, Debra. If you need me for anything I'll be at the bookstore."

Chapter Seventeen

Tyson parked at the back entrance of the bakery. Kara hoped by keeping the front of the bakery in darkness, they wouldn't attract any unwanted visitors. She opened the back door and reached for the wall. Everywhere she looked reminded her of Fred. She blinked rapidly to keep the tears at bay.

Tyson jogged over to disable the alarm. "Is there anything you need me to do before the deliveries come?" The more serious of the twins, he kept his doe-like eyes downcast, seemingly uncomfortable with her emotional state.

She glanced at her watch. "Why don't you scoot over to the diner and grab us both a coffee? I don't feel like putting on a whole pot for just the two of us."

Tyson agreed and rushed out the door. She'd have to get a grip on her emotions. The last thing she needed right now was to lose any of her employees. She raised her hand to knock on the office door and jerked it back. How many instances would there be where she called out his name before realizing he wasn't ever going to be here again?

Kara swallowed a ragged breath and pushed open the door. Fred's baker cap and apron sat strewn across a chair, his runners on the floor, waiting for his next shift. *Should I move them? How would Ada react to seeing them?* Reverently, she picked up the items and put them on the top shelf of the locker they kept their street clothes in.

The back door buzzer sounded. Tyson must have forgotten to flip the lock over on his way out. She jogged through the kitchen and pushed open the door. The smile faded from her face. Noah Steele stood a few feet back from the door with his hands shoved in the front pockets of his jeans, his expression that of a child who was about to be scolded.

"Don't you people ever let up?" Anger erupted. "I have nothing to say to you, Noah. Didn't your brother give you the message?"

"Kara, I had no knowledge my brother was going to do what he did. I would have stopped him if I knew."

He sounded sincere, but she had a hard time believing anything that came out of his far-too-sexy mouth. "I suppose you're going to tell me you didn't know anything about the offer."

He kicked the gravel. "I knew of it, but that doesn't mean I approved."

Tyson rounded the corner of the building, a coffee in each hand. He scowled as he accessed the situation. "Are you okay, Kara?" He shot daggers at Noah in passing.

"Mr. Steele was just leaving." Her heart continued to race as Tyson handed her a coffee.

"I'd appreciate the chance to tell my side of the story." Noah sighed. "I'll be at the bookstore if you're interested."

She quickly looked away, feeling far too vulnerable around this man. "Perhaps another time. We have far too much work to do."

Tyson held the door open for her, all the while giving Noah the evil eye. The young man rocked on the balls of his feet, seemingly ready to pounce if needed.

Without looking back, she slipped into the safety of the bakery, and Tyson closed the door behind him. "Was he giving you a hard time?"

Kara feigned a smile and rubbed her upper arm. "Nothing I can't handle. Thanks for looking out for me."

"Anytime."

The buzzer to the back door sounded off again.

He wouldn't...would he?

"I'll get that." Tyson stepped in front of her.

Kara couldn't help but smile as she watched him assume a fighter's stance before he opened the door. Relief washed over her upon seeing a plump man in a driver's uniform holding a clipboard. She peeked around the driver to the vacant lot.

She wanted to believe Noah had nothing to do with the Steele's desire to buy the bakery. But, even if she did, what difference would it make? There were simply too many unanswered questions. Her focus needed to be on the bakery and helping Ada through this difficult time. She pushed all thoughts of Noah to the back of her mind and busied herself with putting away the supplies.

By five o'clock that afternoon, all the deliveries were unloaded and sorted. Her arms ached from toting around the fifty-pound sacks of sugar and flour. It had been a great release of her building frustration. One she would pay dearly for next morning.

Noah watched Tyson drive past the bookstore with Kara in the passenger seat. He'd spent the entire afternoon waiting in hopes she'd have a change of heart. He put the book he'd feigned interest in over the past half hour back on the rack. *How am I going to get her to see I had nothing to do with what Caleb did?*

Abe had kept his distance from him since he returned from the bakery. Every now and then, he caught him looking his way quizzically. Since this whole ordeal started, Noah hadn't done a lick of his own work. No matter how hard he tried, his thoughts always gravitated to the lovely Kara. Maybe he should just try to channel that energy and get something accomplished.

Resigned and defeated, he turned to his grandfather. "I think I'm going to head on home and try to get some work done."

Abe nodded. "I'm here when you're ready to talk."

Noah shook his head. *The old man is too perceptive for his own good.* He waved, and dashed out the front door, avoiding further scrutiny.

Dark gray clouds hovered above with the threat of more rain. As he made his way to his car, he noticed movement inside the bakery storefront. *Strange...I just saw Kara leaving.* Curious, he strolled over and peeked inside.

Maybe I'm seeing things. He frowned at the empty room, but before he'd turned to leave, he heard a loud bang coming from the back room. Cautiously, he inched his way down the walkway between the bakery and jewellery store. At the edge of the building, he scanned the empty parking lot. Puzzled, he looked up and down the lots on either side before he discovered a familiar car. *What the hell?*

Noah ran to the back door. Seeing the splintered wood on the landing, he pushed open the door. "Hello? Is anyone there?"

The sound of breaking glass assaulted his ears as he stepped inside. He squinted, trying to see through a cloud of white. Not smoke...more like...he licked his lips. *Flour?* A loud crash sent him running through the storage room to the kitchen. Eggs splattered from one end of the kitchen walls to the other. Every glass pane of the ovens smashed.

"Who's there?" shouted Noah.

A figure appeared in the haze, a tire iron held above his head. The dust began to settle and Noah watched as recognition came to the felon's eyes.

"What the hell do you think you're doing?" Noah kept a safe distance.

"I'm giving you one chance to turn and leave. You didn't see anything."

"You're crazy! Do you really think you'll get away with this?" He waved a hand over the destruction.

"I'm warning you: leave while you can."

"Not a hope in Hell. I can't pretend I didn't see this." Noah pulled his cell phone out and flicked it open. He frowned, not able to get a signal.

The culprit loomed toward him. "Who are you calling? The police? " He lifted the tire iron over his head like a sword and sliced through the air between them.

Noah jumped back from his reach. "Why don't you put that thing down?"

"Why don't you kiss my ass?"

Blinding pain exploded on the side of Noah's skull, bringing him to his knees. *He actually hit me.* Noah touched the side of his head, his hand came away sticky and wet. His vision blurred, and the room swam in front of him. He looked up in time to see a metal shelf filled with equipment toppling down on top of him.

Chapter Eighteen

Ada folded to Kara's side as they took in the deliberate destruction of the bakery. The police were called by an unknown source in the wee hours of the morning. They found Noah, unconscious under a utility shelf, a tire iron in his hand, and a twenty pound sledgehammer a few feet away. The police speculated it fell on him while attempting to make a getaway.

Kara had her doubts about him, but never in her wildest imaginings did she think him capable of such an act. Had he sat in wait of her leaving with Tyson before making his move?

Ada sniffled. "I'm so glad Fred isn't here to see this."

Kara rubbed her shoulder. She couldn't think of one comforting thing to say. Determined to stay strong, she repressed the urge to sob.

"Why? I don't understand why?" Her friend appeared so small and fragile in the midst of everything Fred and she worked their whole lives to build.

Kara led her distraught friend to the office. One small consolation was that he hadn't destroyed anything else but the kitchen. "Come, sit down. I'll get you a glass of water."

Her hand trembled as she filled a glass from the sink at the front of the store. Water sloshed over the sides as she walked back to the office to find Ada staring off into space.

"I promised him I'd keep the bakery open, Kara." Her words came out nothing more than a breathy shudder.

Kara shook her head. "I did too." She flopped in a chair across from her. "And that's precisely what *we* are going to do."

Ada pressed her thin lips firmly together, visibly struggling to maintain her composure. She inhaled deeply and stared intently into Kara's eyes. "I don't think there is one piece of equipment that can be salvaged."

"Well, that's what insurance is for. It's long overdue we

upgraded to the twenty-first century anyhow." Even she didn't fall for the positive spin she tried to put on a dire situation.

"It won't happen overnight. The bakery could be closed for weeks...even months."

"Listen, I'm not trying to make light of what happened here, but we might as well make the best of things." She stood and took a pen and paper from the desk. "It will take a few days before the adjusters have sifted through the mess. Why not be ready for when they cut us a cheque. We can shop around for the best equipment while we're waiting."

Ada raised a hand. "Slow down, Kara. I'm not a young woman anymore. I can't get past wanting to know why he did it."

Kara sat back down. "Because they wanted the bakery, and I told them to take a long walk off of a short pier.'

"Why didn't you tell me?"

"Caleb Steele came by the house on the day of the funeral. He offered to buy the bakery since I wouldn't agree to come to work in the Steele Kitchens."

"Oh, dear God." She shook her head. "And this Noah fellow, I thought he was sweet on you. Are you saying he was in on it?"

Kara winced, feeling like someone had stabbed her in the heart. "I wasn't sure until now."

Kara had to be certain. She needed to look him in the eyes and ask him why. The detective in charge wasn't exactly thrilled with her request to visit him in the hospital, but she managed to get her own way.

"There's a guard posted outside his door if you need him. Frankly, I think you're wasting your time. He hasn't spoken a coherent word since we found him on the bakery floor."

She'd spent the day cleaning up some of the debris so the adjusters could assess the damage. Before she went to the hospital, she decided to go home and wash the layer of flour from her body. After being hot and sticky for the best part of the day, she couldn't bear the thought of wearing jeans. She opted for a simple white sundress she'd bought the summer before.

She quickly put her damp hair up in a twist, and then sprayed a modest amount of her only perfume before leaving her bedroom.

"Mom?" Joni called out from her room.

Kara peered around the corner of her daughter's room where she found her laying on top of a beach towel strewn across her bed. "What's up?"

"Where are you off to?" She eyed her up and down.

Kara debated whether to tell her the truth. "I'm headed to the hospital."

Joni bolted upright. "What for? You're not sick, are you? Is it Ada?"

"Relax, nobody's sick. I just need to ask Mr. Steele a few questions face to face."

Joni scooted to the edge of her bed and stood with her hands on her hips. "Oh no you're not."

Kara smiled at her attempt to tell her what to do. "It's something I have to do, Joni. There's no need for you to worry about me."

"Like hell I don't. He's a maniac." She folded her arms across her chest.

"There will be a guard right outside his door the whole time I'm there."

"I'm going with you." She reached for her purse on her dressing table.

"No, you're not." Joni was covered in flour paste from head to toe. "Besides, they won't even let you in looking like that."

Joni looked down at her soiled clothes, and then at the dress her mother wore. She eyed her suspiciously. "What are you really up to? Don't tell me you still have the hots for the guy after what he did?"

"Don't be ridiculous. I'll be home in a couple of hours."

Kara didn't wait for a response and hurried downstairs. Judging by the clock on the wall, a bus would be by in ten minutes. *Perfect.*

She slung her purse over her shoulder and slipped on a pair of sandals. She hated leaving Joni on a sour note, but didn't want to answer any more of her questions. Questions she didn't know how to answer. Thick, muggy air left her drenched in minutes, making her happy she'd chosen the sundress. Thankfully there weren't many people on the bus, probably due to the heat.

It took less than ten minutes to get to the hospital. St. John's was one of the original structures in the city. Big, gray stone walls and courtyards gave it an almost castle feel. Unfortunately, the man lying in one of the rooms was not her knight in shining armour as she'd first hoped.

She purposely took the long way to the front entrance, and strolled through the impeccably kept gardens—vibrant reds and yellows, a startling contrast against the stone. Kara cupped a magnificent red rose and inhaled its essence. A memory of the bouquet sent to the house flashed in her mind.

With her shoulders back, she pressed her lips firmly together and walked in the front doors. She blinked as she adjusted to the fluorescent lights and white walls. A pleasant-looking lady sat primly behind a desk mark, information.

It surprised her to learn he was in intensive care. She pressed a hand to her chest in a futile attempt to slow her rapidly thumping heart. Luckily, the guard posted outside his hospital room door overheard her talking to the nurse.

"I'm sorry, Ms. Walker, but the rules are family only."

The guard stepped forward. "Excuse me. Ms. Walker has been given permission to see Mr. Steele. I can get my supervisor on the phone to verify if you like."

The nurse shook her head and dismissed Kara with a wave of her hand. "You have fifteen minutes, no more."

Kara smiled at the overbearing guard. "Thank you."

He clasped his hands in front and returned to his post beside the door, planting his feet firmly in place.

Kara gently pushed the door open, peeking through the crack to see Noah's sleeping form, a sheet neatly tucked over most of his long frame. His head tightly bandaged and tubes and wires coming and going every which way. A machine behind him made a constant beep.

His eyes were shut. He looked so peaceful despite the bandages and the fact he was in dire need of a shave. Her gaze came to rest on his mouth. Her hand moved to her own mouth where he'd kissed her under the stars on the boat. How could this be the same man? Part of her wanted him to wake, but a bigger part hoped he didn't. How would he try to justify what he did?

Kara perused the room. How odd that he came from such wealth and prestige and the room was absent of any flowers or signs that anyone had come to see him. She sat on a chair at the side of his bed and stared at his sleeping face until a light knock on the door brought with it the nurse.

"I'm sorry, but it's time for me to change his bandages."

Kara lightly touched Noah's hand before she turned to leave. She fought the rush of emotion that threatened to escape. The nurse held the door open and followed her out into the hall.

"Has anyone else been here to see him?"

The nurse shook her head. "His family has been in constant contact by phone, and we have our instructions to call when he wakes up. You are his only visitor other than the police."

"When can I visit again?"

"Our rules are one visitor an hour for fifteen minutes."

"Thank you, Nurse...?"

"Kate. You can call me Nurse Kate."

"My name is Kara. I'll be back a little later this evening."

"You might try talking to him next time. It might help."

"Thank you." Kara made her way to the elevator. It didn't really surprise her that Caleb hadn't been there, but Abe? Her stomach lurched as the elevator made its decent. *What if he doesn't know?* She rushed from the elevator in search of a phone. Just inside the front entrance she found one and fumbled through the phonebook. She keyed in the number.

"Abe's Books."

"Abe? This is Kara Walker."

"Kara? How nice to hear from—"

"Listen, Abe. I'm afraid I have some bad news."

"What is it, Kara?"

"It's Noah."

"Noah? What's going on?"

Kara explained that Noah was in the hospital. He was unconscious but stable. She agreed to wait for him in the coffee shop. Before she went to sit and wait, she called Joni.

"Is he going to be okay?" she asked.

"He's still unconscious."

"Why don't you come home, Mom? There's nothing you can do there."

Kara sighed. "I promised Noah's grandfather I'd stay until he got here. Can you believe no one told him?"

"There's a lot I don't understand when it comes to that family. Promise me you'll come home when he gets there?"

"I'll call you. I know you don't understand why I'm even here to begin with. You're just going to have to trust me on this one."

"Okay, okay. I'm going to go over and sit with Ada. I'm sure she must beside herself over this whole mess."

"I love you, Joni."

"I love you too, Mom. I think you're crazy for being there, but I love you."

Kara hung up the phone, smiling to herself. She really lucked out with a daughter like Joni.

Chapter Nineteen

The term, white as a ghost, took on new meaning as she watched Abe's face visibly pale. "I'm afraid the police say all evidence points to Noah." Kara said, finishing her story about the damage to the bakery

"No." Abe shook his head. "I know Noah better than he knows himself. He wouldn't...no, he couldn't have done this."

"I don't want to believe it either, but the police are convinced he's guilty."

"I don't care what the police say." He grabbed the arm of his chair with a shaky hand and stood. "I want to see him."

"He's still unconscious, but the nurse suggested talking to him." Kara's heart ached. "Do you want me to come with you? He's only allowed one visitor at a time. I already asked, and neither Caleb nor your son has been to see him?"

Abe clicked his tongue. He'd aged ten years since he arrived. "That doesn't surprise me."

He linked an arm through hers, and they made their way to ICU where Nurse Kate smiled from behind her desk.

"This is Noah's grandfather."

"Nice to meet you."

"The name's Abe. Can I bring Kara in with me?"

Nurse Kate looked from Kara to Abe. "It goes against the rules, but as long as you buzz if he shows any sign he's coming around, I'll make an exception this time."

"Understood." Kara tried to convey her thanks her with her eyes.

He leaned heavily on her as they walked past the statue-like guard. Noah lay in exactly the same position she'd left him. Kara led Abe to his side and brought a chair over for him to sit in before she walked over to the windowsill.

Abe pat his grandson's hand. Tears slipped down his haggard

face. “Noah? I think it’s time for you to open those eyes.” His voice cracked, and he took a crumpled hanky from his pocket and blew his nose. “I know it wasn’t you. You need to wake up and tell them who vandalized the bakery.”

Nurse Kate padded across the room with a clipboard in one hand. She went over to the machines and jotted something down before checking the IV tubes.

“How long is he going to be like this?” Abe asked.

“The doctors are hopeful. Keep talking to him. If he can hear you, it might make him fight harder.”

Abe nodded. “Kara, come talk to him.”

“Why me? You’re his family.”

“Yes, I am, but you’re his heart.”

Time seemed to stand still, the incessant beep of the machine echoing the rhythm of her heart. *His heart, how can I be his heart?* Every conceivable emotion grappled in her head as she gazed upon Noah. “Hey.” She brushed a stray hair from his face. “Don’t you dare think you’re getting out of that dinner you owe me.”

His face remained motionless. Kara looked to Abe for guidance. He motioned for her to continue. “You really need to wake up now, Noah. I’m here with your grandfather.”Tears rolled down her cheeks, and she put a hand over Abe’s.

“I’m sorry, but you’re time is up.” Nurse Kate announced from the doorway.

“Maybe it wasn’t him.” Kara said over the rim of the coffee mug she’d been nursing for the past half hour.

“Now, Kara…the police say he did it. I think someone is thinking with her heart.” Ada got up to refill her cup. “Are you ready for more?”

Kara put a hand over her cup. “I’m good.”

“How about we let the police do their job. We have enough to think about putting the bakery back together.”

“The insurance adjusters are going through the place today. We won’t be able to start work until tomorrow at the earliest.”

Kara stood and poured her cold coffee into the sink.

Ada stepped behind her and rested a hand on her shoulder. "You're going back to the hospital, aren't you?"

"I know you think I'm crazy, and maybe I am." She hugged her concerned friend. "I just need to hear it from Noah. I need to find out why he did it—*if* he did it."

Ada sighed. "Get to it then." She walked mindfully from the kitchen, shaking her head.

Without further discussion, Kara left the house to catch a bus to the hospital. She'd spoken to Abe and had agreed to meet him there.

True to his word, as she stepped off the bus, Abe walked toward her. Dark shadows under his eyes told of a night with little sleep. Kara gave him a quick hug. "Has there been any change?"

"I'm afraid not." He replied solemnly.

"Can we sit out here and talk before we head inside?" Kara pointed to the benches in the courtyard.

The morning dew on the blossoms sparkled in the sunlight. Abe took a hanky from his pocket and wiped a place on the bench for her to sit. Kara held his hand and gazed into his tired eyes. "I want you to tell me what kind of man Noah is and why you're so certain he didn't do it."

Abe smiled. "I guess you could say that me and Noah aren't your average Steele men. Zachary Steele, Noah's father, is my son. You wouldn't know it to look at him now, but he wasn't raised to be the kind of man he is today."

"I've wondered why you own a bookstore rather than be a part of the Steele Empire."

"Zachary wouldn't have any of it if he hadn't married Glenda."

"So he married money?"

"In a nutshell, yes." He leaned back against the bench. "They were very happy and very much in love, especially after the boys' births. It wasn't until Glenda took sick things started to change."

"I don't think I ever heard Noah mention his mother."

"If it wasn't for Noah, she would have been put in a home

years ago when she was diagnosed with the early stages of Dementia."

"Noah's father wanted to send her away?"

Abe dabbed at his eyes. "Like I said, he changed, and not for the better. I'm not sure how he did it, but Noah talked his father into letting him and his mother take over a wing of the estate where he would be solely responsible for her care."

"Are you telling me she's still alive?"

"Four years ago, Glenda and Noah moved to the west wing of Steele Estate. My son hasn't visited his wife since."

"Oh, my God, that's awful. Why doesn't Noah just take his mother and leave?"

"Unfortunately, her medical care is quite expensive, and even though it's initially Glenda's money, Zachary has full control of it."

"Now it all makes sense. No wonder you two were so secretive about the Steele name." Kara wrapped her arms around Abe. "I'm sorry." Kara pulled away and pointed. "Look who it is."

Caleb Steele sauntered up the sidewalk to the front entrance of the hospital. He stopped and smoothed his hair in his reflection in the window.

"Maybe Noah woke up." She jumped to her feet. "Nurse Kate told me she was to call them if there was any change in his condition."

Hand-in-hand they rushed into the hospital and up to intensive care. The guard at the door held out his arm to stop them from going into Noah's room. "Sorry, Mr. Steele's brother is visiting; you'll have to wait."

Abe led her to a set of chairs lined up along the wall. Kara stared at the door to Noah's room. Panic rose up within her to the point she couldn't ignore it. "Distract the guard," she whispered to Abe. "Hurry."

Abe ambled over to the guard. "So, who do you think will take the cup this year?"

Kara seized the opportunity. She bolted past the guard and flung open the door. Caleb stood next to his brother, with a syringe containing an unknown substance he'd stuck into his intravenous. “Guard, help!” Kara lunged toward the bed and pulled the intravenous needle out of Noah’s hand. She had no idea what was in the syringe, but she just knew it wasn’t good.

The guard flew into the room just as Caleb threw the syringe under the bed and bolted for the door.

“He tried to kill him!”

The guard grabbed Caleb’s arm and pulled it up behind his back. “I saw you throw it under the bed. Do you want to tell me what it is?”

Nurse Kate rushed in and over to Noah’s side. “Will somebody please tell me what is going on here?”

Kara had her fingers pressed over the spot where the needle came out to stop the blood.

Caleb squirmed as the guard snapped handcuffs around his wrists. “There’s a syringe under the bed. This man was shooting it into the IV when Kara pulled the needle out of his hand.”

Kara stared intently into Caleb’s eyes. “Why? He’s your brother for God’s sake.”

“If you had just accepted my offer, none of this would be happening. It’s your fault, bitch.” He spat.

“It was you, wasn’t it? You destroyed my kitchen, didn’t you?”

Caleb threw his head back and laughed. His raspy cackle echoed the madness in his eyes. “Do you really think my perfect, do-gooder brother could have done it? I had to do something. Now you have no choice but to take my father’s offer.”

Kara walked right up to Caleb as he struggled against the confines of the handcuffs. “When Hell freezes over, Mr. Steele.”

Caleb jerked toward her, but was quickly reined back by the guard. “Okay, that’s enough. You and I are going to take a little ride downtown.”

“You ruined everything...you fucking bitch! I’ll get you for this...nobody messes with a Steele!”

Abe held the door open. Caleb didn’t even acknowledge his presence as he was ushered out the door. Disgusted, he shook his head.

Kara turned to Nurse Kate. “Is he going to be okay?”

“Thanks to you, I think so.” She knelt down and scooped the syringe from under the bed. “I’ll send this down to the lab and find out exactly what this is.” She held the needle in one hand and unhooked the intravenous tube with the other. “I’ll be back to hook up another IV. “Thank God you got here in time to stop that madman.”

Chapter Twenty

Despite the excitement at the hospital, Noah remained in a deep sleep. Kara kept herself busy with getting the bakery back up and running. She stepped back to admire the wall she'd just painted. Tyler and Tyson spent the day clearing the room of all the damaged appliances and debris. It had been a royal pain in the ass cleaning up the flour. Water and flour made paste, and using the broom just made a bigger mess. Tyler ended up renting a shop-vac to suck it all up.

"How long before the new rotating oven is delivered?" Joni stepped down from the ladder with paintbrush in hand.

"It's supposed to be here by the weekend." Kara rolled her roller in the tray.

"What about the supplies he ruined?"

"I re-ordered. Some will be here tomorrow, and the rest on Thursday."

"So when do you think we can open?"

Kara laughed. "Aren't you full of questions today?" She left the roller in the tray and grabbed a bottle of water. "If everything goes as planned, I think we can re-open on Monday."

"That's terrific. I'll let the twins know." Joni joined her mother.

"Let's take a break and sit out front for a bit."

Lunch hour brought a steady stream of traffic down Main Street. Occasionally a car would honk and the driver waved to them. Down the street, customers entered and left the bookstore. Abe had shortened the hours the store was open so he could devote more time to Noah. He'd started reading to him in hopes Noah would hear him.

Kara's thoughts were with Noah constantly, but she'd made a promise to Fred, and she fully intended to keep it.

"I still can't believe he tried to kill his own brother." Joni shook her head.

“When you think about it, he tried to kill him twice. He all but left him for dead here.”

Joni drank from her water bottle. “What will happen to Caleb now?”

Kara shrugged. “He’s been charged with attempted murder and a number of other charges for what he did here. I don’t think we have to worry about him for quite some time.”

They sat in amiable silence. Once the painting was done, she’d go home to clean up, check in with Ada, and go back to the hospital.

“Do you think Noah will be okay when he wakes up?”

Kara swallowed hard. She asked herself the same question every day. “There’s no way of knowing. We’ll just have to wait and see.” She blinked back the tears that threatened to fall.

“I wonder why his father hasn’t come to see him.”

Kara shook her head. Joni would be heading off to college in the fall, but at times like this, with all her questions, it was a little girl with pigtails she remembered. “From what Abe tells me, they aren’t very close. The only reason Noah still lives on the estate is to take care of his mother.”

Kara had searched for information about Dementia. Given the progressive deterioration of her memory, she wondered if Glenda even knew who Noah was. The thought had crossed her mind to pay her a visit, but she didn’t want to chance upsetting her.

“He is going to make it...he has to.”

Joni put an arm across her back and squeezed her shoulder. “Of course he is.”

Abe sat next to Noah’s bed, reading from a book on his lap. Nurse Kate had relaxed on the rules since the incident with Caleb, and the fact they were Noah’s only visitors. Kara smiled at Abe as he looked up from the book.

Abe pat Noah’s hand. “Look who it is. Kara has come back to see you.”

Noah remained motionless.

"No change?"

Abe shook his head.

"Let me read to him for a bit. You go stretch your legs."

Abe smiled and put a bookmark in the pages where he'd let off. He stood up and rounded the end of the bed. "Thank you, Kara. I don't know how I would have got through this whole ordeal if it wasn't for you."

Kara gave him a hug and kissed his cheek. "That's what friends are for."

"Would you like me to bring you back a coffee?"

Kara picked up the book. "How about a nice cup of tea?" Her jaw dropped. "You're reading him a romance novel?"

Abe laughed "It's one of his favourite authors." He opened the door. "I won't be long."

His Loving Embrace, by Adam Love. "Go fig." She observed his sleeping face. Someone had given him a shave. She feathered her fingers down his smooth jaw line. Her heart wrenched. "Hello handsome. It's me, Kara." She leaned over and pressed her lips to his cheek. "Don't you think it's about time for you to wake up? You still owe me a dinner, remember?"

She sighed and eased herself onto the chair, opening the book where Abe had left off just as Nurse Kate strode in the room.

"Well, good evening, Kara." Nurse Kate smiled and put her two fingers on Noah's wrist to take his pulse.

"Hi, how are you?"

"I'm good, thanks." She wrote on the clipboard at the end of his bed. "The results came back from the lab about the contents of the syringe."

"What was it?" Her pulse quickened.

"Heroin. Enough to get every patient on this floor high for a week."

"Heroin? That son-of-a-bitch wasn't taking any chances, was he? Where in the hell did he get hold of that?"

"If you have enough money, you can find anything you want." She checked the IV. "If you didn't pull this out of his hand, he would have O.D.'d in a matter of seconds."

Kara felt the color drain from her face. If she hadn't acted on her gut feeling...Noah would be dead.

"Are you okay, honey? You look a little pale."

"I guess I never realized just how close he came to dying."

Nurse Kate smiled. "I'm sure Noah will thank you when he hears what happened."

"Honestly, do you think he'll be okay?"

"I don't know. But he's breathing on his own, which is definitely a good sign." She fussed with his sheets before heading for the door. "Oh, before I forget, his father called today asking about his condition."

"How generous of him to take the time to pick up the phone." Kara's words dripped with sarcasm. Even the mention of Zachary Steele turned the contents in her stomach sour. She shuddered.

Nurse Kate pulled open the door. "If you need anything just push the buzzer.

"Thanks."

Kara settled back in the chair and opened the book. She scanned the page before she started to read. She read a few pages before realizing she'd been keeping rhythm with the steady blip of the machine at the head of his bed.

Is this how our life together will be? She stood and searched his face for answers. How she yearned to see his beautiful brown eyes, to have them look at her like she was the only other person on the planet. She took his hand in hers, resting his palm against her cheek, feeling his warmth. "I'm sorry...I'm sorry I ever doubted you."

She laid her head against his chest, comforted by the lull of his beating heart. Abe's untimely return interrupted the intimate moment. Kara pulled away from Noah, heat rushing to her cheeks.

"I'm sorry, I didn't mean to intrude." He handed her a steaming cup, the tag from the tea bag dangling over the side.

"Thank you." She motioned for Abe to sit, and she leaned against the window ledge. "I wondered, since Noah is here, who is taking care of his mother?"

"She has a private nurse and a housekeeper. I imagine they've been informed and are taking care of everything."

Kara had never laid eyes on Noah's father, but from everything she'd heard, compassionate wouldn't be a word to describe him. "You don't think your son might put her in a home now that Noah isn't there?"

Abe stopped blowing on his tea. "To be quite honest, the thought never crossed my mind."

"Is there someone you can call to make sure she's okay? I'm sure Noah is going to ask about her when he wakes up."

"I'll make some phone calls when I get home. It's no wonder Noah was so infatuated with you. You're one of a kind, Kara Walker."

The rhythm of the machine they had grown so accustomed to changed tempo. Kara's heart jumped to her throat. They rushed to either side of Noah searching for a hint of difference. Kara fumbled with the buzzer as they watched the tape reading whirl in a frenzy; the jagged lines etched a new pattern across the screen.

Noah's eyelids wrinkled and smoothed, his lashes fluttered. His mouth opened a crack and a burst of air released.

Nurse Kate rushed into the room. "What's going on?"

Kara pointed to the tape. "I think he's trying to wake up." Her eyes brimmed.

"Please step back a minute." She read the tape and quickly checked his pulse. Her eyes grew big. "Could one of you go out and ask the nurse at the desk to page Dr. Stouffer?"

Kara bolted for the door. The nurse behind the desk jumped to her feet.

"Call the doctor." Kara gasped. "Call Dr. Stouffer now. Noah is waking up!"

Chapter Twenty-One

Throughout the night, Kara drifted in and out of sleep. The doctor confirmed the increased brain activity and ordered his pain medication reduced to almost nothing. If Noah was trying to wake, he wanted to make it easy for him to do so.

"Sometimes these things take time." Dr. Stouffer looked over the rim of his glasses. "We'll keep a close eye on him. Try not to say anything that might upset him." He turned to Kara. "But it wouldn't hurt to remind him there are people who care waiting for him to open his eyes."

That was over six hours ago. Nurses came and went at fifteen-minute intervals to check the readings, but he still hadn't opened his eyes. Tired and frustrated, she sat on the edge of the bed facing him. She'd persuaded Abe to leave about an hour ago to shower and get some rest.

Kara rest her head on Noah's shoulder, and inched closer until her lips almost touched his ear. "Noah, you have to come back to me. You're the man I dreamt of as a little girl." She didn't think she had any tears left to shed, but several trickled down her cheeks. "I'm sorry for doubting you."

"Mom?"

Kara jerked upright, wiping the tears away. Joni stood in the doorway with picnic basket in hand, her face lined in worry.

"Joni, I didn't hear you come in."

"Is everything okay?" She stepped toward her.

"Yes. What do you have there?" Kara slipped off the edge of the bed.

"I thought you might be hungry."

Kara's stomach grumbled as the aroma of fried chicken wafted toward her.

"I brought fried chicken and a little cheesecake."

"Did someone say cheesecake?" Abe entered the room.

Kara laughed.

"There's plenty for both of you." Joni set the basket down on the window ledge. As she opened the lid, the scrumptious aroma filled the room.

The steady blip of the machine picked up its tempo. Kara, Joni, and Abe, exchanged a look of shock.

"Quick, give me some chicken." Kara held out her hand while Joni opened the container and passed it to her mother. She took out a piece and waved it under his nose. The machine kept up the escalated rhythm, but he remained motionless. She prayed for a sign, any sign, Noah was waking. "Joni, did you say you brought cheesecake?"

"What are you going to do?" she asked, as she stood next to Kara holding the dish.

Kara dipped her finger in the creamy filling. "They say the way to a man's heart is through his stomach." She parted his lips and rubbed trace amount on the tip of his tongue.

Slowly his mouth closed, and she watched as his jaw moved, his lips parted to reveal the clean tip of his tongue.

"Oh, my God...I think he wants more." Kara put a little more filling on his tongue. This time his cheeks sucked in and his Adam's apple moved when he swallowed.

Abe stood on the other side of the bed. "Noah? Open your eyes for me. It's Gramps."

Noah's eyelashes flittered. His lips parted and barely above a whisper, spoke the most beautiful sound. "More...." He looked out half open lids.

Kara laughed and cried. "Oh Noah, you stay awake and I'll make you cheesecake every day, for the rest of our lives." She placed her hand in his, rewarded by his fingers curling around her hand. The corners of his mouth lifted ever so slightly; his eyes closed, fingers relaxing.

"Joni, go get the nurse!" Kara searched Abe's face. "Why isn't he staying awake?"

"These things take time." Abe took a crumpled hanky from his pocket and blew his nose. "He's coming back to us, Kara. We just have to be patient."

Kara hated having to leave the hospital, but no way could Ada handle all the deliveries by herself. The new mixers and kneaders were coming in, and she needed to be there. The rotating oven had been delivered before she arrived. What a thing of beauty it was.

If everything went as planned, they'd be open for business on Monday. Abe had closed the doors to the bookstore until further notice. She'd relieve him whenever she could so Noah was never left alone. The bell above the front door chimed.

"Deliveries come in the back." Kara called out as she made her way to the front of the store. She stopped in her tracks. Without being introduced, she knew she was looking at Noah's father. Dressed in a perfectly tailored suit, he wore an expression of steel as their gazes locked.

"Ms. Walker, I presume?" He extended a hand. "Zachary Steele."

Kara had no desire to shake this man's hand. She matched his frigid stare until he withdrew his hand and let out heavy breath.

"I think we've gotten off on a bad note." He bowed his head slightly. "Please accept my apology for my son's actions."

"I'm rather busy, Mr. Steele. Is there a reason for your visit?"

Kara watched Noah's father struggle to keep his anger in check. It was obvious he wasn't used to not having the upper hand.

"I heard you were going to re-open the bakery. I wanted to see for myself."

"No thanks to your son, Caleb. We will be re-opening on Monday." Kara walked passed Zachary Steele and opened the door. "So if that is all, I really must be getting back to work." Kara's heart raced as she fought to appear much more self-assured than she actually felt.

"You know, Ms. Walker, it really isn't necessary for you to go to all this trouble. My offer still stands. We'd be happy to have you come to work in our Kitchens."

"Save your breath, Mr. Steele. I'm sure your kitchen is state of the art, but there's one thing I have here that you will never have there."

Zachary Steele eyed her warily. "And what would that be?"

"Heart." Kara stood tall, never prouder to be a part of Fred and Ada's bakery. "That's something your money can't buy."

"Maybe you aren't right for my kitchens after all." He jutted his chin and walked past her out the door.

"You know, the past weeks I've spent at your son's bedside, I felt sorry for him. I can't imagine how hurt he's going to be when he learns his own father never once came to see him."

Zachary Steele glared down at her, anger flashing in his eyes. "You know nothing about my relationship with my son."

Kara shook her head. "I know enough now that it's not Noah I feel sorry for, it's you."

"I don't have to stand here and listen to this. Good day, Ms. Walker." His chauffer opened the door of the limo, and Zachary slipped inside.

Chapter Twenty-Two

Frustrated, Kara slammed the phone back in its cradle. She tucked her towel securely above her breasts and plunked herself down at the kitchen table. She'd been so busy with the bakery opening, there didn't seem to be enough hours in the day to get everything done, including time to visit Noah.

Every time she called the hospital the night before, and just now, a different nurse answered the phone, none of them Nurse Kate.

"I'm sorry, Miss, but we can only give out that information to immediate family." Kara mimicked.

Thankfully the twins agreed to hold down the fort while she went to the hospital this morning to find out what the hell was going on. She drained the last of her coffee and climbed the stairs to dress. She chose to wear jeans and a t-shirt so she could go straight to work from the hospital. With her damp hair plaited down her back and a quick swipe of mascara, she dashed out to catch the bus.

"Oh crap." She groaned upon seeing the packed bus. There was standing room only, and Kara was forced to stand between two middle-aged men. One of which smelled like he'd just bathed in a vat of tuna. Her eyes watered as she was pushed even closer to the stranger. The balding man frowned and turned, giving her a bird's eye view of his attempt to take a few longer strands of hair and comb them over to hide the barren patch. A burst of heat rose up between them, accompanied by the most God-awful smell. Mortified, she put a hand over her nose and mouth. *Did he really just do what I think he did?*

The bus stopped, and the foul stranger turned to walk to the exit, but not before meeting her gaze and grinning from ear to ear. Rendered speechless by the audacity of the man, she shook her head and glared back at him.

That settles it. I am buying a car!

Finally, the bus stopped in front of the hospital, and she bolted for the door. Outside, she took a few cleansing breaths before entering the building. A familiar, full-bodied aroma lured her to the coffee shop where she bought a large, dark roast to take with her to the ICU. Her heartbeat quickened as it always did at the prospect of seeing Noah. She took a steadying breath before stepping off the elevator. Nurse Kate wasn't at the nurses' station. Instead, a middle-aged woman with a not too friendly demeanour narrowed her eyes at her.

Kara feigned a warm smile. "Good Morning. I'm here to see Noah Steele."

"Mr. Steele is no longer with us."

Her words robbed her of breath, and she held onto the counter to keep herself from falling. Tears sprung to her eyes and she swallowed hard. "I don't understand."

Concern replaced the nurse's stone face, and she hurried to her side. She took Kara's arm and ushered her to a chair. "I'm sorry, what I meant was that Mr. Steele's family has made arrangements for him to be cared for at home."

"Took him home?" Kara searched her face for answers. "Who did?"

"I really don't think I'm at liberty to say, Miss. Rest assured, he is getting the proper care. In fact, his family hired one of the nurses from here to care for him."

"Nurse Kate?"

"Why, yes." The phone on the desk rang. "Now, if you'll excuse me."

Kara stared down the barren corridor. A million unanswered questions whirled in her mind. *By family, did she mean Abe? Is that why I haven't been able to reach him? Surely it wasn't Noah's father who took him home, or was it?* She jumped to her feet and gripped the counter.

"Please, can you tell me how I can reach Nurse Kate?"

The plump woman put a hand over the mouthpiece of the phone. "I'm afraid I can't give out that information."

"If I give you my name and number, will you please have Nurse Kate call me?"

She pressed her lips firmly together and shook her head before handing Kara a pad of paper and pen.

Kara scrawled her name and phone number for the bakery and home. "Thank you." She ran toward the elevator, glancing inside the room she spent many countless nights reading to Noah. A crippled old man lay sleeping in his bed. Furious, and more than a little confused, she blinked back tears.

Noah.

Kara upset a metal tray filled with utensils, scattering them in all directions.

"Shit!" Kara kneeled, picking up the utensils with one hand and wiping away tears of frustration with the other.

A gentle hand on her shoulder unraveled the last thread of her resolve and she slouched down and sobbed. "Why hasn't anyone called to tell me where he is? I just don't understand."

Ada persuaded Kara to her feet. "Now, now. Come sit in the office and have some coffee with me."

Kara leaned on her friend and they crossed the kitchen to the office. Joni's and the twins' looks of concern followed them.

"I'm so sorry, Ada. I'm just so worried about Noah."

Ada brushed back the hair from her face. "Look at it this way, Kara. Noah must be doing well for them to okay his release home."

Her ragged breath permeated the room. "I guess you're right. I'd feel a whole lot better if I knew where he was."

"It's only been a couple of hours, Kara. I'm sure Abe or Nurse Kate will call soon."

Kara took the tissues offered her, blowing her nose noisily. She let out a heavy sigh. "You must think I'm being silly."

"Not at all. Maybe you should go home and try and get some rest."

Kara noted the concern in her voice. How selfish was she to inflict her petty insecurities on a woman who just lost the love of her life a few short weeks ago. “No. I’m sorry Ada. I’ll be fine now.” She straightened her posture and forced a smile. “Besides, we still have much to do if we are going to be ready to open Monday.”

For the remainder of the afternoon, Kara made a concerted effort to keep her mind off of Noah. They were able to finish the painting, set up the equipment, and were now putting away the last shipment of supplies they had reordered. All the while, the phone on the kitchen wall remained silent. She checked her messages at home a few times with no news of Noah’s whereabouts. Something wasn’t adding up.

“Ready to take a break?” Joni put a hand on Kara’s shoulder just as she set the phone back in place.

“Sure.”

“Are you hungry? Tyson and Tyler were thinking we’d order some pizza.”

“That sounds good. You go ahead.”

Ada came out of the office. “Did you say the twins were going for pizza?”

Kara saw the dark circles under her friend’s eyes and realized the toll these long hours at the bakery were taking on her. “You know, I think we can handle things here. If you want to go home, they can drop you off on the way.”

Ada failed to hold back a yawn and laughed. “If you’re sure it’s okay.” She put a hand to the small of her back. “These old bones could use a long soak in a hot tub right about now.”

Joni kissed the top of her head. “The twins are leaving in about fifteen minutes, okay?”

A smile rejuvenated the old woman’s face. “You’re a good girl, Joni. I’ll just go change my shoes and grab my purse.”

Kara gave Ada a heartfelt hug and the twins left with her to pick up supper.

“Let’s sit out front and wait for them to get back.”

“That sounds like a good idea.” Kara followed her daughter outside. Supper hour brought a welcome lull to Main Street.

“You know, I’ve been thinking about Noah.”

"You and me both." Kara sighed wearily.

"No, I mean about where he is. If Abe took him home, he would have called you by now, don't you think?"

Kara shrugged.

"Also, do you really think Abe could afford to hire a nurse and everything else involved to take care of him outside of the hospital?"

Kara's heartbeat accelerated. Her daughter's words rained new light on the situation. "What are you saying, Joni?"

"I can only think of one man who has the kind of pull and money it takes to make something like that happen."

Kara's eyes grew big as it became clear to her. "Zachary Steele."

"None other."

"But why?"

Joni shrugged. "Control."

It all made sense. Kara knew for certain the one thing in Zachary Steele's life he strived for was control. That was the main reason he tried so hard to buy the bakery and her services. Since he failed, he must be royally pissed off at her. What better way to make her pay.

"Son-of-a-bitch!"

Chapter Twenty-Three

The last time she'd been this pissed off, a Steele man was behind it. Only it wasn't Caleb this time; it was his father. If she acted on impulse, she'd have ended up in jail for assault. Luckily Joni talked her into going home and sleeping on how to best approach things. If Zachary had Noah at the estate, running off half-cocked would have served no purpose. If she learned nothing else, she'd learned the head of the family was big on proper procedure. So, under the pretence of a prospective famous pastry chef wanting to join the Steele Kitchens, she made an appointment to see the man the following afternoon at Steele Towers.

After tossing and turning most of the night, she stood under a cold shower to chase the cobwebs from her mind. She couldn't help but feel a little guilty about abandoning Ada when the re-opening was only two days away. They had all assured her things would be fine as long as she could spend the entire next day preparing her desserts for the big day.

Kara sat at her dressing table, adding the finishing touches to her make-up. She wanted to look as professional as possible when dealing with Zachary. Joni had loaned her a pale lavender blouse to wear with her black dress pants and she wore her hair up in a rather severe bun to complete her no-bullshit persona. She put a pair of small pearl earrings on and sprayed a cloud of perfume of which she walked into. "Ready or not, Mr. Bigshot, here I come."

As promised, Tyson sat out front to drive her to Steele Towers. It would be a cold day in Hell before she'd get on another bus after her last experience. Kara hopped up into the passenger seat and held her stomach to calm the butterflies fluttering around inside. Luckily she managed to curb her anger. No good could come of her losing her cool. She only hoped the man didn't say something to set her off.

"Are you okay?" asked Tyson as he slipped into mid-afternoon traffic.

Kara let out a shaky breath. "I have to be."

"Do you want me to come with you?"

The threat of tears snuck up on her. *Since when did I become such a cry baby? It's high time I cut it out, right here and now. I'm not giving the almighty Steele the satisfaction of seeing me in tears. In fact, it's high time the man learns exactly what kind of woman he's dealing with.* "That's very nice, Tyson, but I think this is something I need to do alone."

He shrugged and kept his eyes on the road. "If you need me, just call."

"Thank you." Kara replied as she rolled her neck and straightened the crease of her pants.

Steele Towers loomed ahead. He pulled the truck up to the main entrance. "Give me a shout at the bakery when you're ready to leave."

"I will." She leaned over and kissed his flushed cheek. "Thanks for everything."

Kara shielded her eyes from the sun as she gazed up at the building's side. Zachary Steele's office was on the top floor. She took a deep breath before entering the lobby. Everywhere she looked, money was evident from the highly polished marble floors to the oversized paintings that hung from expertly textured walls. Her heels clicked against the expensive tiles as she crossed the lobby to the elevators. The doors mysteriously opened without having to push a button. A man dressed in a black suit ushered her inside.

"What floor, Miss?"

"Zachary Steele's office."

"Very good." He jabbed the button labelled PH.

The elevator moved as if on air, unlike any elevator she'd ever ridden. There was no sudden movement that made her stomach lurch. The doors opened, and the man accompanied her over to a room with only one desk. Seated behind the polished wood sat a stern-looking woman with a phone to her ear. She held up a finger as Kara approached her.

Kara waited while the woman finished her call. At either side of the elevator, seating areas filled with high-back armchairs and glass coffee tables. A series of magazines fanned across the surfaces. Instead of pictures on the walls, brocade fabric hung in padded panels.

"Can I help you?"

The secretary pulled her attention back. "Yes, I have an appointment with Mr. Steele."

The woman opened a leather bound planner. "Your name?"

"K...Diane Stanley." Kara forced herself to remain calm despite her heart racing in her chest.

"Please be seated, Mr. Steele will be with you in just a few moments."

Kara offered a week smile to the tight-lipped woman and made her way to the seating area. She pulled up the sleeve of her blouse to reveal a bare wrist. *Damn.* She surveyed the room for a clock. Despite the absence of one, the longer she sat there, the louder the seconds became. Absentmindedly, she flipped through a magazine; her gaze flitted to the only set of doors at the far end of the reception area.

"Ms. Stanley, Mr. Steele will see you now."

Kara jumped in her seat. She grabbed her purse and towered over the petite secretary.

"Right this way."

Kara followed the woman, forcing herself to remain calm. She opened the door and stepped aside, allowing her entrance. Zachary Steele sat behind a large wooden desk, his eyes widening.

"Diane Stanley I presume?" His brows arched and he steepled his fingers under his chin.

The door closed behind her, and she inched toward the desk. "I'm sorry about that, Mr. Steele. I didn't think you'd grant me an appointment if I used my real name."

"You thought right." He straightened and waved to an empty chair. "Ordinarily I'd call security and have you escorted from the premises, but I must confess to being intrigued by your audacity, and more than a little curious as to why you are here."

Kara sat at the edge of the straight-back chair. "I think you know why I'm here."

"Humour me." He sneered.

"I went to the hospital yesterday. Imagine my surprise to find Noah had been taken home to recover." Kara struggled to remain calm as she noticed the corners of his mouth lift into a look of smugness.

"And just why is that any concern of yours? I can assure you he is receiving the best of care."

"Let me guess. You have him tucked away in the same wing as your wife?"

Color stained Zachary Steele's cheeks, his eyes ablaze. "How dare you talk of my wife."

"Listen, I need to see for myself Noah is okay. Do I have your permission to see him?"

Zachary tilted his head back and laughed. "You are the most infuriating woman I have ever met. You insult me and ask my permission in the same breath. I can't think of one good reason why I should let you come and see Noah."

Kara lifted her chin and looked directly into his eyes. "Noah would want me there."

He shook his head. "Did he tell you that?"

Kara felt heat rush to her cheeks. "Not in so many words."

Zachary checked his watch. "Your time is up, Ms. Walker, unless of course there is something else you wish to discuss."

Kara was on her feet, no longer able to contain her anger. "You are the most cold, unfeeling animal I have ever met in my lifetime, and I've met some winners in my day. I bet you don't even remember forcing me to uproot my daughter and move to the city."

"If you're talking about the sale of your house in the country, I can assure you it was simply business. Maybe if you had kept better track of your husband's finances, you wouldn't have found yourself in such an undesirable position."

"How dare you! No wonder your own father wants nothing

to do with you. Doesn't it matter to you what your son wants?"

Zachary stood. Anger flashed in his eyes. "When my son is well enough to tell me what he wants, then I will listen. Until then, I can assure you he will be well taken care of. As for my father, if he hates me so much, why has he moved to the estate? Good day, Ms. Walker."

Kara spun on her heel, not trusting herself to stay a moment longer. *So that's where Abe has been. Some way, somehow, I'll find a way to see Noah. You can go straight to Hell, Zachary Steele.*

Chapter Twenty-Four

Angry gray clouds hovered above Kara, echoing her mood. The thought of calling Tyson for a ride back to the bakery hadn't even entered her mind. Her only thoughts were of putting as much distance between her and Zachary Steele as quickly as possible. Never had she met a man like him. In some ways he acted more like a spoiled child than a multi-millionaire. It was as if he were punishing her for not jumping over to the Steele side. He even managed to get Abe under his roof. *How?*

The only thing she knew for sure was that she had to find a way to see Noah. A crack of thunder brought with it the onslaught of rain. *Perfect*. Kara turned up the flimsy collar of her blouse in a futile attempt to keep the rain from completely soaking her. She laughed in spite of herself and quickened her pace, fully aware of the glances from men and women safely under the protection of umbrellas.

"Good day." Kara waved at a young couple. "Nice day if you're a duck." Her voice dripped with sarcasm, and the two quickly shifted their gazes from her.

The bakery came into view about the same time the clouds parted and the sun came out. Kara reached the store and sank down onto the bench, not ready to face the onslaught of questions everyone inside was bound to ask.

Warm sun on her damp skin chased away the chill. There was so much to do in the next forty-eight hours to prepare for the re-opening, and all she could think about was Noah. The bell above the door tinkled, warning her she'd been spotted.

"Mom?" Joni stood with her hands on her hips. "What on earth are you doing? You're soaked. Why didn't you call for a ride?"

Kara held up a hand to stop her daughter's rant. "I'll tell you everything, but later. Right now, can you ask one of the twins to run me home so I can change?"

Concern filled her daughters' expression. "Are you okay?"

Kara feigned a smile. "I'm fine. Now go."

Noah eased open his eyes and tried to focus in the dark room. The curtains were drawn, but a sliver in them told him it was daytime. It didn't take long to realize he was no longer in the hospital. A machine beeped from behind him, and an IV came out of his hand. *Why did they take me from the hospital?* He lifted his head, and the room began spinning so he eased back on the pillow. His tongue felt thick and dry as he tried to work up enough moisture to swallow. A memory of the taste of cheesecake made his stomach growl and his heart ache.

"Kara," he whispered hoarsely.

He squinted against the sudden flood of light. Blinking rapidly, he focused on the silhouette in the open doorway.

"Well, hello there." Abe beamed at his grandson.

"Gramps?" Noah rasped, his throat on fire. "Water?"

Abe scurried to his bedside table and took an ice chip from a Styrofoam container. He held it to Noah's parched lips. "Let it melt in your mouth."

Noah closed his eyes, revelling in the coolness of the ice as it filled his mouth and slid down his throat. "More."

Abe smiled and held another ice chip to Noah's lips.

A picture of Caleb holding a tire iron over his head flashed in his mind. "Caleb?"

Abe pat his hand. "Don't worry about any of that right now. We know what your brother did."

Noah's heartbeat quickened. "Kara?" He envisioned her warm lips pressed to his cheek on several occasions.

"Kara is fine."

Noah's eyelids became too heavy to hold open. He wanted to ask so many questions but he couldn't fight the darkness that overcame him as he succumbed to sleep once again.

Kara came back to the bakery after changing. Before anyone had a chance to ask her anything, she gathered them in the kitchen.

"As you all probably know, Noah is no longer in the hospital. The nurse on duty wouldn't give me any information about his whereabouts other than the fact Nurse Kate had been hired to care for him." Kara took a steadying breath. "So, I went to see the almighty Zachary Steele, only to find he'd moved Noah to the estate and I'm not welcome there."

"Oh, Kara, I'm so sorry." Ada shook her head.

"Thanks, but here's the real kicker. Abe moved to the estate as well. Needless to say, my walk home in the rain was fuelled by an overwhelming desire to commit bodily harm."

"My God, this whole ordeal is just crazy. I didn't think Noah's father cared." Joni pressed her lips firmly together.

"I don't think Noah is home because dear old Dad had a compassionate moment. I think he's trying to get back at me for turning down his offer." Kara's temperature began to rise yet again. "For now, we have a lot of work to do before Monday morning. If Nurse Kate is with Noah, I don't have to worry about him. Let's get to work. I'm sure I'll think of some way to see him after the celebration."

"Well, you're right about one thing: we do have a lot to do." Ada walked over to Kara's side and squeezed her shoulder. "It will all work out, Kara. I'm sure of it."

"Thanks." Kara clapped her hands together. "Okay then, I'll get the cheesecake started. It can be refrigerated and topped later on." Kara motioned to the twins and Joni. "You three need to pick up the big coffee makers from the Rent-All center. We'll need coffee cups, napkins, and small plates for cake. Speaking of cake...Ada, if you don't mind, you can help to make the slab cake. If we can get all of this done today, then tomorrow we'll busy ourselves with pastries and bread making. I have a feeling we're going to need a ton of it."

Like a well-oiled machine, they set off to complete their tasks. Kara couldn't be happier to be busy. It kept her mind off of breaking into the estate. She'd driven by the Steele Estate before. Large iron gates were manned by a guard who sat in a small booth to one side. Cameras turned at regular intervals atop large stone pillars. There was no way she'd be able to *break* in; she'd have to be a little more creative. She dumped several bricks of cream cheese into a large mixing bowl and set the machine in motion.

Maybe she'd get lucky and Nurse Kate would get her message to call. Kara couldn't help but wonder why Abe hadn't phoned. He had to know how worried she'd be. Undoubtedly, Zachary had something to do with it as well. Kara nodded decisively as she measured out sugar. *Well, Mr. Steele, I'm afraid you don't scare me. I'll find a way to see Noah, whether you like it or not.*

Chapter Twenty-Five

A decidedly feminine scent filled his senses, nudging him awake. *Kara.* His heartbeat skipped, and he opened his eyes to see the stark white uniform of a nurse leaning over him. He coughed.

"Oh." The nurse put a hand to her chest. "Mr. Steele, you startled me. I'm Nurse Kate."

Noah watched her check his IV, noting she had kind eyes. "Water?"

"Of course, Mr. Steele." Nurse Kate scooted to the other side of the bed and put an ice chip to his mouth. "How do you feel about sitting up today, Mr. Steele?"

Noah frowned. "Please, call me Noah."

"Of course, Noah." She reached for a set of controls dangling over the side of the bed. "Now I'm going to bring the bed up a little at a time. You tell me if you start to feel light-headed at all, okay?"

He smiled and grabbed hold of the sides of the bed. Slowly, he assumed a sitting position. His head pounded, but he didn't feel the all-too-familiar sensation of falling back to sleep. Once he grew accustomed to sitting, the pounding subsided.

"Okay?" she asked.

"Yes."He shifted his attention to the ice container.

"More?" She smiled broadly. "How about we try some clear soup today?"

Noah's stomach grumbled at the mention of food, and the nurse laughed causing heat to rush to his cheeks.

"Well that's a good sign." She winked at him. "The grumble *and* the blush. I'll be back in just a minute."

No sooner had she left than his grandfather scuttled into the room.

"What a nice way to start the day. Nurse Kate told me you

were sitting up. How do you feel?"

Noah noticed the dark circles under his eyes. He hated that he might be the reason for his lack of sleep. "Hungry."

Abe slapped his knee. "Now you're talking!"

"Why am I here?" He asked, more confused than ever.

His grandfather sighed like he'd been dreading the question. "Your father arranged for you to come home."

His brow arched. "My father? Home? Why are you here then?"

Abe shrugged. "I guess he figured it was easier than trying to stop me."

Noah smiled. "Kara...is she here too?"

Abe's smile faded and he shook his head. "No. She was at your bedside everyday when you were in the hospital, but your father won't let her come here."

Noah's temper flared. "He won't *let* her?" He huffed and clenched his fists. "I want to see him...now."

"I'll try to get a hold of him. You need to calm down." Concern lined his weathered face.

Noah relaxed his hands and made a concerted effort to appear calm for his grandfather. "I'm sorry, my father is an ass."

"I can't argue with that." He offered a weak smile that failed to mask the hurt in his tired old eyes.

"How is Mother?"

"Still the same—happy in her own little world."

Nurse Kate appeared in the doorway with a bowl of soup. "Now let's see how you do with some nice warm beef broth. Maybe we can get rid of that IV today."

Noah nod his approval, determined to build up enough strength to get out of bed. The sooner he was up, the sooner he could go to Kara. Damn his father for keeping her from him.

At four in the morning Kara had trudged from a bed she'd tossed and turned in for most of the night to Tyler's waiting truck and an extra-large coffee. Despite the fact that the clock now only read noon, she felt like she'd already put in a double shift. At least she'd made considerable progress. She only had the cheesecake to top and cut into squares and a few trays of tarts to fill to finish up all of the pastries and desserts. The twins had all four racks filled with cooling bread and buns in the ovens. They saved one batch to put on first thing in the morning so the bakery held the scent of fresh-baked bread.

Kara leaned on the front display case and took in the room. Fred must be smiling down on them all. Ada worked her magic in creating the most beautiful cake to welcome their customers back. Never had she known a stronger woman. Not all women who had just lost their husband and best friend of fifty years could rally the strength needed to re-open the bakery.

Luckily, she'd been able to sneak in a phone call to ensure her surprise would be ready on time. She'd been planning it since the day she made her promise to Fred. Her bottom lip quivered as she repressed a barrage of sentiment.

There will be plenty of time for tears, Kara Walker. There's still a lot of work to do.

Joni pushed open the front door and rushed inside toting bags of ribbon and balloons. "Did someone say there was going to be a party?" She threw her head back and laughed.

Kara laughed along with her highly contagious mood. "Now what have you done?"

"You can't have a proper party without balloons, can you?"

"I guess not, but if you think I'm going to blow up one of those balloons, you're nuts."

Joni spoke out one side of her mouth. "That's why we have two strong men in the kitchen, plenty of hot air."

"Oh dear." Kara shook a finger at her. "You better not let them hear you, or you'll be blowing them up by yourself."

"Nah, neither one of them can resist my womanly charms." She fluttered her eyelashes.

Kara snapped her daughter's backside with a towel. "Get on with ya, you cheeky devil."

Joni disappeared through the swinging doors just as the phone rang. Kara jumped as she had been doing all morning. She wiped her hands on her apron and picked up the receiver.

"Hello?"

"Kara, is that you?"

Relief washed over her upon hearing Abe's voice. "Yes, oh Abe, I'm so glad you called."

"I don't have a lot of time to talk."

"Okay, how is Noah?"

"He's doing well, Kara. He's sitting up in bed for the first time and Nurse Kate is feeding him some soup as we speak."

Kara closed her eyes and tilted her head upwards. *Thank you, God.*

"Kara? Are you still there?"

"Yes," she sniffled. "I'm so pleased. I wish I could come and see him."

"I know, honey, I'm really sorry about that, but I had to agree not to contact you in order for my son to let me stay with Noah."

"I thought something like that had happened." She summoned up the courage to ask the question weighing heavily on her mind. "Has he asked about me?"

Abe chuckled lightly. "Yes, about five seconds after he opened his eyes."

Kara choked on a sob. "I'm so glad you called. Please tell him I would be there in a heartbeat if it were at all possible."

"I will Kara. I better let you go. I'm not sure when or if I'll be able to call you again anytime soon."

"I understand. The bakery is re-opening tomorrow morning, so can you tell Noah? I think that will please him."

"It pleases both of us. Congratulations!"

"Good-bye, Abe."

"Kara?"

"Yes?"

"I love you as if you were my daughter...you know that, don't you?"

The emotion she heard in his voice enveloped her like a warm embrace."Yes, I love you too." She said and the line went dead.

Chapter Twenty-Six

Kara slipped under a blanket of bubbles. The warm water soothed her tired bones. They had finished everything they possibly could at the bakery by five o'clock. Now she had the entire evening ahead of her with nothing to do but nurse her aching body. It seemed she'd been riding an emotional rollercoaster forever. Abe's phone call today had done wonders for her disposition.

Noah is okay and he asked about me.

How am I going to get past all that security to see Noah? Even if she did manage the astronomical feat, where would she go once inside? The estate covered the equivalent of six city blocks. Abe had told her that Noah and his mother lived in a wing of their own, but was that where his father was keeping him?

Kara sighed wearily and pulled the plug before she stepped out of the tub and dried off. The soft fabric of her full-length bathrobe caressed her. She couldn't remember the last time she had the house to herself for the evening. Joni and the twins had decided to go chill out at the drive-in.

Downstairs in the kitchen, she put the kettle on the stove to boil and opened the fridge. She wrinkled her nose, seeing nothing appealing. *Maybe there's something good on television.* Her bare feet squished in the plush living room carpet. Simple pleasures. The book she'd been reading to Noah sat on the coffee table. *Imagine a man like Noah enjoying a good romance novel.*

She flipped the book open and leafed through the pages, her attention caught by a small photo on the inside jacket flap. Puzzled, she held the book open under the light.

"Noah?" Kara assessed the picture of Noah's twin, only in the picture his hair was down. She skimmed over the brief bio. *Adam Love lives in the big city, inheriting his love of books from his grandfather. When Adam isn't writing or reading, he cares for his ailing mother.* "Well, holy crap!" Kara laughed out loud. "Never in a million years...!"

The whistle on the kettle blew simultaneously with the ring of the phone. Startled, Kara dropped the book and fumbled for the receiver.

"Hello?"

"Hello, is this Kara?"

"Yes."

"Hi, this is Nurse Kate returning your call."

"Oh, I'm so glad you called."

"I'm so very sorry for everything. I just finished talking to Abe. What kind of monster is Zachary Steele?"

"You have nothing to be sorry for." Kara stretched the phone cord out as far as it would go, her fingers skimming the controls on the stove. She briefly held the phone from her ear and silenced the whistling kettle. "I hear Noah had a good day today?"

"Better than good. We started the day by having him sit up and eat some soup. By supper time he was demanding fried chicken and cheesecake of all things." She laughed. "I'm afraid we'll have to tie him down soon to keep him in bed."

Kara laughed, thrilled to hear of Noah's progress. "That's wonderful."

"How fast can you get to the hospital?"

"Why?"

"Do you want to see Noah?"

Kara's heart raced. "Of course I do, but how?"

"I'll explain everything when you get here. I figure I better bring you to Noah before he makes a run for it to see you. I'll be at the nurse's station in ICU."

Kara hung up without saying good-bye and darted for the stairs. In record time, she dressed in jeans and a t-shirt, threw her hair up in a clip, and slipped into a pair of runners. She was out the door before she remembered her last ride on the bus, and nobody was around to give her a lift. Mumbling to herself, she went back inside and called a taxi.

Although the cab came right away, it seemed to take forever

to get to the hospital. For someone who didn't want another man in her life, she was sure in a hurry to see one. Kara threw all caution to the wind the moment the taxi stopped and tossed the driver a twenty-dollar bill for an eight-dollar fare and bolted from the car. Upon entering the hospital, the halls were eerily quiet. As much as she wanted to run, she didn't want to be thrown out before she met with Kate.

For what seemed like an eternity, she waited for the elevator and then again for a rather lengthy ride up to ICU. By the time she made it to the nurses' station, she feared she might burst. Nurse Kate looked up from her paperwork, the corners of her eyes crinkling.

"Wow, you got here fast."

Kara's cheeks warmed, and she smiled while shifting from side to side. "You said I can see Noah?"

Nurse Kate put a finger to her lips. "I'll just be a quick second, and then we can get started." She winked and motioned for her to take a seat.

Kara stepped back from the counter and sat in a chair against the wall. She could hardly believe she was going to see Noah. Her curiosity was definitely piqued as to how. Luckily for Kara, Kate was true to her word and rounded the counter with purse and sweater in hand. She linked her arm through Kara's and led her toward the elevators. Before they made it that far, Kate took a quick look over her shoulder before nudging Kara into the janitor's closet.

"What on earth are you doing?" Kara whispered in the dark.

"Shh." Kate felt along the wall and flicked on the light. "We don't have much time." She started taking off her uniform. "Quick, we need to trade clothes."

Kara complied without question. Within minutes, she was twisting her hair up under Kate's cap. Kara was surprised to see how young Nurse Kate looked out of uniform. Her jeans were a little long on her, but other than that, a perfect fit. She tugged down the uniform skirt.

"It's a little shorter on you than me, but I'm sure Noah won't mind one bit." She giggled. "When we get downstairs, there will be a car waiting to take you to the estate. Don't worry; it's been a different driver every night. When you get there, a butler of sorts will be waiting at the door to take you to Noah's room."

"Surely he'll notice I'm not you." The prospect of being found out unnerved her.

Kate squeezed her hand. "I think you can pull it off; besides, we've never once exchanged two words. He'll walk ahead of you to Noah's room and magically reappear at exactly eight thirty to bring you back to the front door where a car will be waiting to take you back to the hospital. I'll keep a look out for you from the parking lot and I'll drive you home from there."

Kara's heart pounded so hard surely Kate heard it.

"Just stay calm and keep your head down. You'll be fine."

She took a shaky breath "If you say so." They rode the elevator down by themselves. Just before it stopped, Kate squeezed her hand.

"You're on your own now. Good luck and I'll see you back here shortly after eight thirty."

The doors opened before Kara had a chance to respond. Kate walked ahead of her out of the hospital. True to her word, a driver waited out front with the door open. Kara tried to appear shorter by slouching down. Without any words exchanged, the driver closed the door behind her.

Kara welcomed the silence in the Sedan to pull herself together. She wiped her moist palms on the plush seat cover. It would be at least a fifteen-to-twenty-minute ride to the estate. Excitement and apprehension filled every recess of her being. If she did manage to pull this off, she owed Nurse Kate a huge debt of gratitude.

What if after all this Noah is asleep? She said he had a good day, but what if all the exertion tired him? Kara forced herself to stop second-guessing. *In just a few minutes, I'll see Noah. Nothing else matters.*

Chapter Twenty-Seven

Noah stared at the blank page, his muse MIA. How could he write romance when the woman who won his heart wasn't even allowed near him? Anger festered in the pit of his stomach, tainting his love for her. *I have to find a way to see her.*

For as far back as he could remember there had been sibling rivalry between him and his brother. At what point did Caleb start hating him enough to want him dead? In fact, if it wasn't for Kara's quick thinking, he would be.

"Knock, knock."

His grandfather came into the room. The smile on his face faded upon seeing the state his grandson was in. "Oh boy. What's going on in that head of yours?"

Noah grimaced as he pulled himself up to lean against his pillows. "Is it that obvious?"

"If it were any more obvious, there'd be a gray cloud over your head." He sat on the edge of his mattress. "What's on your mind?"

"I can't wrap my brain around what Caleb did. What did I do that was so unforgiveable he'd want me dead?"

Abe sighed. "I think your brother's problems run much deeper than any of us knew. He'd become almost obsessed with needing your father's approval. You and Kara weren't making it very easy for him to do that, and he couldn't handle it."

"Why didn't he see that no matter what we do, it isn't ever going to be good enough for our father?"

He shrugged. "Maybe he didn't want to see it."

A deep sadness enveloped him.

"Listen, Noah. There's no making sense of your brother's actions. He wasn't thinking rationally, and because he wasn't, he'll be gone for a very long time."

Do you know what the kicker is about this whole mess?" He looked sideways at his grandfather.

Abe shook his head.

"You can bet your ass that my *father* hasn't lost one wink of sleep over any of it."

Noah saw the conflict of emotions dueling behind his kind old eyes. Sometimes he forgot that his father was also his grandfather's son. "I'm sorry, Gramps."

Abe shrugged and drew in a ragged breath. He took a crumpled hanky from his pocket and turned away to blow his nose. "I think we could both use a good night's sleep. Can I get you anything before I turn in?"

"You go ahead. The nurse will be by shortly to tuck me in."

His grandfather snickered and walked toward the door. "Maybe if you ask real nice, she'll read you a bedtime story."

"Very funny." Noah smiled and lay his head back on his pillow and closed his eyes–a flashback of Kara at his bedside, her moist lips pressed against his cheek...her salty tears on his lips. Somewhere along the way, they'd crossed the invisible line between friendship and something more.

How can my father keep her away from me? Especially knowing it was her who saved my life? He'd forgiven his father for many things, but this? As soon as he was able, he'd move from the estate and take Mother with him. There had to be a way to do so without causing her too much stress.

The door to his room creaked and he opened his eyes to see the nurse's familiar white uniform. The only light in the room came from his bedside table. "Come to tuck in your favourite patient?"

"I guess you could say that." She murmured.

Nurse Kate stood at the end of his bed in the shadows. There was something different about her tonight. He squinted. Why hadn't he noticed she had killer curves going on? His jaw dropped and his pulse quickened as she stepped out of the shadows. She put a hand to her white cap and let loose a wave of fiery red hair.

"Kara."

She smiled broadly as she rounded the bed and sat at his side. Her beautiful blue eyes were glistening pools. He held out his arms, and she pressed her warm body against his. In all of his thirty-seven years, he'd never felt anything so incredibly...right.

Noah kissed the top of her head, inhaling her sweet essence. "I'm so sorry."

Kara lifted her head, her face a mere whisper from his. "You have nothing to be sorry for. I don't have much time. Let's not waste it."

Noah cupped the side of her face. "Thank you." He swallowed hard, surprised by the single tear he felt roll down his cheek. "Thank you for saving my life."

He drew her to him and pressed his lips to hers. Her body relaxed, and she laid her head on his chest, half lying on the bed with him. There were no words, the love between them, palpable.

"I'm so happy to see you." She spoke softly against his chest.

"I'm sorry you had to go to such lengths, but I'm not sorry I got to see you in that sexy nurse uniform."

Kara laughed huskily. "So it's true. You *are* feeling better."

He kissed the top of her head. "Much better now that you're here. How long do you have?"

Kara glanced at her watch and sighed. "Only another fifteen minutes."

"Damn my father."

Kara lifted herself so she hovered above him. "Soon you will be well and we can see each other as often as we like." She rained kisses down his nose, ending at his mouth.

"I think I'm all better now." He grinned. His hardened member pressed firmly against her thigh. "How can I let you go?"

"You will close your eyes and have sweet dreams. I will be waiting for you when you are well enough to come to me."

Noah put a hand on each side of her face and stared deeply into her eyes. If he learned nothing else through this whole ordeal, it was life is too damn short to leave things unsaid.

"I love you, Kara Walker."

Her eyes filled, and her fell lips glistened. "I love you too."

Kara stepped out of her clothes and slipped into a nightshirt.

The plan had gone off without a hitch, and she even made it back home before Joni. Her fingers traced the outline of her lips, unable to wipe away the smile. She sat at her dressing table, noting the rosy glow to her cheeks and the sparkle in her eyes.

To think that not long ago the only thing on her mind was how she would cope once the summer was over and Joni had left for college. Now, she knew for certain, no matter what path her future took, Noah would be a part of it.

Would it be possible to love this man without his father's negativity infiltrating their lives? They'd find a way; besides, not all of the Steele men were so bad. Abe and Noah were nothing like Caleb and Zachary.

A beam of light illuminated her window for a fleeting moment. *Joni must be home.* Kara tip-toed to the window and looked down to see Tyson's truck parked out front. It was several minutes before the driver door opened, and he hopped out, jogging over to the passenger side and opening the door for Joni. *Good boy.* Kara smiled as she watched Tyson walk her daughter to the door and kiss her soundly before dashing back to his truck. Kara's heart skipped a beat. Her little girl wasn't so *little* any more. She sighed. If Joni wanted to see someone seriously Kara whole-heartedly approved of Tyson.

Kara darted back to the dressing table. The front door slammed shut, and she stifled a giggle. *Spying on your own daughter...shame on you.*

Joni's footsteps grew closer until she stood in the doorway, her cheeks stained pink.

"How were the movies?"

Joni shrugged, unable to look straight at her. "Okay."

"You mean, what you saw of them were okay."

Joni rolled her eyes. "What are you talking about?"

"You and Tyson."

Her daughter's cheeks reddened. "So what did you end up doing this evening?" Joni was quick to change the subject.

"Nothing much." She ran the brush the length of her hair. "I just impersonated a nurse and snuck into the estate to see Noah."

Joni's jaw dropped. "Are you serious?"

Kara laughed. "Yes and I'm happy to report, Noah is doing much, much better."

"I swear I don't know you anymore." She shook her head. "Do you have any idea how much trouble you would have been in if you'd been caught?"

Kara sighed. "It was so worth the risk."

"Am I nuts, or are you seriously in love with this guy?"

"Be happy for me, Joni." Kara pleaded.

"Oh, I'm happy for you. I think you're bonkers for getting involved with that family, though."

"They're not all bad. Besides, I'm seeing Noah, not his father."

"If you say so." Joni shrugged. "Just be careful. I don't trust that man one bit."

"Don't you worry. I have both eyes wide open."

Joni yawned. "Well, I'm going to bed. We have a big day ahead of us tomorrow." She walked over to the dressing table and kissed her cheek.

"You got that right." Kara reached up and gave her a hug. "I love you, Joni. Good night."

"I love you too. See you in the morning."

Chapter Twenty-Eight

Kara woke up before the alarm went off, totally stoked about the day ahead of her. She hadn't been this happy in a very long time. A big part of it had to do with her visit with Noah, but also, she would be fulfilling her promise to Fred today. They all worked their asses off to get everything done in time.

Quietly, she dressed and tiptoed down the hall to the bathroom so as not to wake Joni. There was no reason for her to get up at four in the morning. If she made it to the bakery by eight, she'd have plenty of time to get things started for the grand re-opening.

The full-bodied aroma of coffee wafted toward her as she made her way downstairs. Thank goodness she remembered to set it before going to bed. Lights flitted past the front window signalling Tyler out front to pick her up. She filled her to-go mug and raced for the door before he had a chance to knock.

"Good morning. Ready to roll?"

"You betcha. It's going to be a great day!" Kara closed the door behind her and checked to make sure it locked. "Is your brother already at the store?"

"Yup, he has the first batch of bread in the ovens."

"What's got into him? Is he sick?" Kara sipped her coffee.

Tyler shrugged. "Not sure, but he was already at it when I got there this morning."

"I'm sure going to miss you guys when school starts."

They drove through the sleeping city to the bakery in an amiable silence. Kara went over her mental checklist of things to do before nine. She smiled broadly, remembering the surprise she had planned. *Now if I can just pull this off without Ada suspecting anything.*

Since they were so ahead of the game and only needed to get some bread baked, Kara opted to take care of loading the pastries and desserts into the showcases. Usually Joni and Ada took care of it, but she found herself actually enjoying the task. It took over two hours to get it all out, but when she finished and looked around at all they'd accomplished a sense of pride filled her.

A truck pulled up out front of the store, and Kara squealed with delight. She checked her watch before rushing out the door. "Right on time, gentlemen."

Two middle-aged men in overalls got out of a pickup and plodded over to her.

"Can you get it done in half an hour?"

The taller of the two looked up, shielding his eyes from the sun. "I think so."

"Great, and you're going to cover it like we discussed so no one can see it before the unveiling?"

"Yup." The two men answered in unison.

"Great. Now I just have to find a way to keep Ada from sneaking a peek." Kara laughed, feeling very sneaky indeed.

Kara left the two men to their work and went directly back to the kitchen.

"Which one of you is picking up Ada this morning?"

Tyson looked up from filling pans with dough. "That would be me, Ada *and* Joni."

"Terrific. I want you to make sure you bring them in the back door."

He exchanged a puzzled look with Tyler. "Why?"

"Never mind why, just do as I ask, okay?" Kara winked.

Tyler shook his head and laughed. "Uh-oh, what are you up to?"

"I'd tell you, but then I'd have to kill you." She spun on her heel and strode back to the front of the store to check on the men's progress.

"Don't play me for a fool." Zachary Steele paced the length of Noah's bed. "I know what happened last night."

Noah grinned sheepishly. He visualized Kara's long legs in a very short nurse's uniform.

"You think this is funny?" The veins on his father's neck bulged. His face turned redder by the moment. "How dare she try and pull one over on me!"

"You didn't really leave her much choice."

"I told her once you were able, I'd ask if you wanted to see her. Was that good enough? No!" He shook his head vigorously. "I've had it up to here with little Ms. Kara Walker and her holier-than-thou-attitude. Just who in the hell does she think she is?" His hand sliced through the air above his head.

"Calm down, Father. It's not like she did anything so terribly wrong. Like it or not, I plan on seeing a lot more of Kara, so you might want to get over this obsession you have with her."

"Obsession? Is that what you think it is? If it wasn't for that woman, you wouldn't be in that bed recovering from a coma and Caleb wouldn't be behind bars for possibly the rest of his life!"

"You're insane. None of that is Kara's fault." Noah tried to sit, but fell back on his pillow. He searched the side of his bed for the controls. "How is she responsible for my little brother trying to kill me?"

"She pushed him over the edge." Spittle sprayed from his mouth. "Caleb would never have done something like that if she hadn't made him feel like he had no other option."

"That's just crazy talk." Noah let out a rush of breath. "Is the nurse here yet?"

"Nurse? You mean the one who helped your little trollop sneak in last night. You don't really think I'd keep her after that, did you?" Zachary stormed over to the door. "Your grandfather will see to your needs now that you're out of danger." He threw open the door and left.

Seconds later, Abe ran into the room. "What the hell is going on? I haven't seen him this angry since he found out that you write romance novels."

Noah sighed. "He found out Kara snuck in here last night with Nurse Kate's help."

"Is that why he told me I'd be taking care of your needs from now on?"

"Yup, he's really lost it this time. He blames Kara for Caleb being in jail and me being in this bed."

That's ridiculous." Abe shook his head in disbelief. "Where did he storm off to just now?"

Noah shrugged. "I don't know. I'm just glad he left."

Abe frowned. "Well there's not a whole lot we can do about it now. Let's just concentrate on getting you out of that bed."

Noah glanced at his bedside clock. "Yes, the sooner, the better."

"I'll be right back with some breakfast." How does porridge sound this morning?"

He scrunched up his face. "Yuck, I haven't had porridge since I was a kid."

"Well, it's either porridge or toast. I never claimed to be Betty Crocker." He winked.

"How about a little of both? I'll pretend I'm eating steak and eggs." He fumbled with the remote to raise himself to sitting up. "I'd like a phone as well."

Abe stopped and looked over his shoulder. "Do you want your father to fire me?"

"Either you bring me a phone, or I'll crawl to get one." Noah countered

Abe held up a hand in surrender. "Okay, okay, don't get your undies in a knot. Breakfast first, and then I'll figure out a way to get you a phone."

Chapter Twenty-Nine

Kara checked and rechecked her watch every five minutes. The store opened in less than half an hour and Tyson still hadn't returned with Ada and Joni. A nagging sense of foreboding prickled up her spine. She rubbed her shoulders and rolled her neck as she walked to the back door and opened it wide.

"Where the hell are they?" Kara said to the barren lot. She zipped through the supply room to the kitchen. "Does your brother have his cell phone with him?"

Tyler put the last tray of buns on the rack to cool. "He should have."

"Do me a favour and give him a call. Find out what's taking them so long."

"Sure thing." He wiped his hands on his pants and grabbed the receiver from the phone on the wall.

She tapped her foot impatiently, checking her watch yet again. *Something's wrong. I just know there's something wrong.* The back door slammed shut. A very concerned-looking Tyson approached, followed by Ada.

"Where's Joni?" Kara glanced at the empty space behind Ada.

"I was hoping she'd be here. We went to your house and she isn't there."

"What do you mean she isn't there?" The feeling of something amiss shifted to full-blown panic.

"Well, I knocked and waited a few minutes. When she didn't answer, and since the door wasn't locked I went in and checked." He shrugged. "She wasn't there, Kara."

"Did you say the door was unlocked? I made sure I locked it behind me." Her gaze darted from Tyson to Ada.

Ada scurried to her side and rubbed her back. "Now let's not get upset, I'm sure she just had to stop somewhere before coming in. She'll be here at the last minute, you'll see."

Kara rubbed her upper arms. “It's not like Joni to be unaccounted for. She knows how I worry.”

“She's not a little girl anymore. Let's keep busy, and I'm sure before you know it, she'll be here.”

Kara nodded, although unable to shake the sense that something was terribly wrong. Of all the mornings to break routine and not peek in her room, she had to pick today. For all she knew, she could have been gone since the middle of the night.

“What still needs to be done?” asked Ada.

“The coffee....setting the table with cups and napkins, cream and sugar. Oh, and balloons and streamers are in the office.”

“We'll take care of the decorations.” The twins chimed in together as they often did.

Kara noted several people standing outside waiting for the open sign to appear in the window. Joni's unexplained absence stole her excitement. The phone rang, and Kara dove across the room to answer it. “Joni?” she asked breathlessly.

“Kara?”

Kara slouched against the wall. “Oh, Noah. It's so nice to hear your voice.”

“You sound worried. Where's Joni?”

The concern in his voice touched her heart. “I'm not sure. It's probably nothing.” Kara drew a steadying breath. “In less than ten minutes we are scheduled to re-open the bakery, and Joni is nowhere to be found.”

“Are you saying she's missing?”

“Well, not exactly missing. She's unaccounted for. Tyson went to pick her up this morning and she wasn't there.”

“I'm sure she's fine. Maybe she has a surprise up her sleeve.”

Kara laughed a nervous laugh. “You're probably right.”

“Look, I just wanted to wish you congratulations on the re-opening of the bakery.”

“Thank you, Noah. I miss you already.”

“I miss you too. I better let you get back to work. Can I call you later to hear about Joni's surprise?”

She smiled. “You can call me anytime.”

"Kara, the crowd is getting restless. Can we open the doors now?" Ada stood at the front door.

Kara hated to start without Joni, but she couldn't make the customers wait any longer. She crossed the room and put an arm around her waist. "I have something to show you first."

"Can't it wait? Look at everyone out there."

"You boys clear a path out there. I have something to say before we open for business."

The twins, who were lurking just outside of the kitchen doors, sprung to action. "We're on it."

"Trust me." Kara steered a puzzled Ada out the door.

A round of applause greeted them. Tyson and Tyler parted well-wishers until Kara and Ada stood in front of the boisterous crowd.

"If I could have your attention for a moment." Kara shouted over the crowd and waited until the noise subsided. "I'd like to thank you all for coming to the re-opening of the bakery. It saddens us that our dear Fred isn't here to join in the celebration. I like to think he is smiling down on us right about now."

Ada dabbed at her eyes with an embroidered hanky.

"We made a promise to Fred that we'd keep the bakery open. I want to take it one step further." She reached behind her and felt for the rope. "I want to make sure everyone knows it is because of Fred this bakery even exists."

She passed Ada the end of the rope. "Will you please do the honors?"

Ada's tear-filled eyes followed the rope up to a tarp. She gave the rope a tug and the tarp fell to the ground. The sign above the window read. Fred's Place, in a fancy scroll—across the bottom...Home Baked Goodness. Tears spilled down Ada's flushed cheeks. "Oh, Kara. How wonderful."

A thunderous applause reverberated down Main Street. Kara wrapped her arms around Ada's thick waist, allowing her own tears free rein.

Noah's suspicions grew with each passing minute. *Joni is*

missing...my father's over-the-top outburst this morning... Coincidence? No, he wouldn't, would he? "Gramps!" Noah summoned all his strength to slide his legs over the side of the bed. His muscles were like jelly from lack of use. "Argh!"

"Easy now. What's got you all riled up?" Abe rounded the bed to stand at his side.

"I need to see my father now!" He inched his way to the side of the mattress.

"You try to stand and you'll end up flat on your face."

Noah punched the mattress in frustration. "Joni is missing."

"What? Are you sure?"

Noah rubbed his unshaven jaw. "Kara is worried sick."

"And this has what to do with you demanding to see your father?"

"My gut tells me he has something to do with it. He's not thinking straight and holds Kara accountable for everything. What better way to make her suffer than through Joni?"

His grandfather seemed to age before his eyes. "Do you really think your father is capable of doing something like this?"

Adrenaline coursed through Noah's veins. "Don't you? Listen, there's a wheelchair in my mother's suite, will you help me?"

Abe searched his face. "Where do we start?"

Noah stroked his stubbly jaw. *That's it!* "Jeffery. My father doesn't take a shit without him knowing." Noah unbuttoned his pyjama top. "Leave me a change of clothes and go get that chair, okay?"

Abe hurried from the room, returning a couple of minutes later with a neat pile of clothes. "Do what you can. I'll help you when I get back."

The simple task of taking his top off left him breathless. *This is no time to cave, man. Kara and Joni need me.* He gritted his teeth, and, with renewed determination, he put an arm through the armhole of his t-shirt. Now, with both arms through, he sat for a second, summoning the strength to pull it up over his head. With every strained movement he garnered a new respect for the disabled. He managed to get his head through the neck hole, but that's where he stopped, the muscles of his arms on fire.

Abe came through the door pushing a wheelchair. "It was already out in the hallway."

Noah shrugged. "You're going to have to help me." He huffed, sweat dripping from his forehead. "I think a two-year-old has more strength than I do right now."

"Don't worry. Before long you'll be back to your old self. These things take time."

The steady stream of customers kept all four of them hopping, but no matter how busy it got, Kara's concern for her daughter continued to grow. She replayed over a hundred scenarios in her mind, but none of them made any sense. Every few minutes, she noticed Tyson check his cell phone for messages.

At around two in the afternoon, the traffic in the store waned enough for her to duck back to the kitchen where Tyson replenished a tray of rolls. "Hey Tyson, when you were at my house this morning, do you think it's possible you might've overlooked a note from Joni?"

Tyson looked up at her and shrugged. "I went upstairs and checked all the rooms while Ada looked downstairs. If there was a note, don't you think one of us would've noticed?"

Kara chewed her thumbnail. "Maybe, but maybe not. Did you notice if her bed was slept in?"

"I dropped her off last night, Kara. I promise I made sure she made it inside safely."

"Of course you did. I'm grasping at straws here." She peeked between the swinging doors. Ada tended to a customer while half a dozen people lingered throughout the store. "Would you mind going by the house and taking a better look around?"

"Sure. I'm starting to get a little worried myself."

Kara took her purse out from a cubbyhole under the counter and rifled around for her keys. "Here are my keys. Maybe you could leave a note for her to call if she reads it."

"Good idea." He took the keys and untied his apron. "I'll try not to be gone too long."

"Thank you." If he didn't come back with good news, she'd start calling hospitals.

Chapter Thirty

Noah and Abe hit one brick wall after another. Zachary Steele wasn't anywhere on the estate. A quick check in the garage to find all cars accounted for had them both perplexed to say the least. Not only didn't they find his father, but the entire estate seemed to be void of staff.

"It looks like he gave everyone the day off." Abe scratched the top of his head.

"Why would he do that?" Noah frowned. His eyes opened wide. "Unless he was up to something he didn't want anyone to know about."

"Where the hell is he?"

"I know one thing for sure: he isn't alone. Wherever my father is, you can be sure Jeffery isn't too far away."

Abe put up a finger. "Maybe you should give Kara a call and see if Joni's turned up yet."

Noah retrieved his cell phone wedged between his thigh and the wheelchair. "Keep your fingers crossed."

The phone barely started to ring when it was picked up.

"Joni?" Kara blurted.

"Kara? It's Noah. I'm just checking to see if you'd heard from Joni, but I guess you haven't"

"Tyson just left to check out the house again. He's going to look and see if there's a note from Joni anywhere. He'll leave a message for her to call me if she does show up." Her tone bordered hysteria. "I don't know what else to do, Noah."

"Well, I didn't want to say anything, but I had a talk to my father this morning."

"You did? What did he have to say?"

"He knew all about you sneaking in. He fired Nurse Kate too. He blames you for everything, and I mean everything."

"Oh, my God! You don't think he's done anything to Joni, do

you?"

Noah let out a breath. "I didn't say that, but something isn't sitting right. It's all too, coincidental."

"I'm coming out there right now!"

"Now hold on just a minute. We just searched the entire estate and we can't find my father."

"Noah, you shouldn't be out of bed."

"Don't worry, my grandfather is pushing me around in one of my mother's wheelchairs."

He heard her sniffle. "Please don't cry, Kara. We'll find her. Listen, I just had a thought. I'll call you back real soon, okay? You hang tight in case she calls."

"What are you going to do? You can't expect me to do nothing when there's a chance Joni is in trouble!"

Noah shook his head, regretting having told her of the altercation with his father. "I'll make you a deal. If he isn't where I think he might be, I'll come and get you. We can look together, okay?"

"Please be careful."

"Don't worry. Nothing is going to happen to me."

Noah flicked his phone off. "Damn! Why did I say anything to her?"

Abe shrugged. "Doesn't much matter now. The cat's out of the bag. You said you had a thought?"

"Yes. The only place we haven't checked is the west wing."

"You don't really think he'd take Joni there, do you? He hasn't been anywhere near there since you and Glenda moved in."

"Exactly. He thinks I'm still in bed, and it would be the last place anyone would think to look for him."

"You might be onto something." Abe took hold of the wheelchair and turned it towards the west wing. "One question, though. What do we do if we find him and he has Joni?"

Noah wrung his hands. "I have absolutely no idea."

Abe wheeled him down the corridor toward Noah's wing of the Estate. Suddenly the chair jerked to a stop, almost toppling Noah out of it. His grandfather's hand covered his mouth as he pulled him backwards the way they came.

"Hush." Abe stooped down to Noah's level.

"What the hell is going on?" Whispered as loud as he dared.

"I just saw Jeffery coming out of your place. He's headed toward your father's office."

"No shit? If that bastard hurt my mother...." Anger encompassed him, and he clenched his teeth. He tried to move the wheelchair forward but his muscles refused to respond. "We can't just leave; we have to find out what they're up to."

Abe squeezed Noah's shoulder and turned his wheelchair around. "I'm an old man, Noah. What do you want to do? Ambush them? Run them down with your wheelchair?"

More than half an hour passed since she talked to Noah. Kara practically jumped out of her skin every time the phone rang. *Could Zachary Steele be so vindictive to take Joni?*

Tyson came in the back door and jogged to the kitchen. Kara searched his face expectantly. He stooped over with his hands on his knees, gasping for breath. "Nothing...no note...no Joni...."

Panic seized Kara with an iron fist. "We have to go to the Steele Estate." She snatched her purse from the counter.

"What?"

Kara took hold of his arm and practically dragged him to the exit. "I'll explain on the way there."

"Kara?" Ada called out from behind her. "What's going on?"

"I'll call you later, Ada. I'm sorry but I have to go..." Kara didn't even look back. She pushed the bar and swung open the door with Tyson still in tow.

"Easy now." Tyson pulled his arm away.

"I'll drive." Kara ran to the driver's side of Tyson's truck.

Tyson nudged her aside. "I don't think so. I want to get there in one piece."

She cast him a sideways glance and realized he wasn't joking around. "Okay, but we have to hurry."

They boarded the truck, and he peeled out of the parking lot. "Now are you going to tell me what this is all about?"

Kara sat at the edge of her seat. "Noah thinks his father might have Joni."

"What? Why would he think that?"

"Because he's a vindictive control freak and he thinks I'm to blame for Caleb being in jail and Noah...." Kara buried her face in her hands. "If that son-of-a-bitch hurts her, I swear, I'll kill him."

Tyson turned down the road where the estate began, the main gate still a good distance away. "So tell me...once we get there, how do we get in?"

"There has to be a way." Kara silently prayed she was right.

The ominous black iron gate loomed before them. The small building where the guard usually sat, stood empty.

"Now what?" He gripped the steering wheel and looked from left to right.

Kara bolted from the truck and jiggled the gate to no avail before running over to the guardhouse. She pulled at the door to find it locked. She searched the grounds before picking up a rock by the roadside, and proceeded to heave it at the window. The glass spidered, but didn't break.

"Here." Tyson handed her a wrench out the window of the truck.

Kara took the wrench and smashed the fractured pane, rewarded by it raining glass to the ground. Carefully, she reached in and unlocked the door. Inside, she saw a small panel with a red lever switch.

"Please let this work." She pulled the lever, and the iron gates groaned and inched open. She looked up at the sky as she ran back to the truck. "Thank you."

Chapter Thirty-One

Noah snapped his phone shut. "Shit." Ada wasn't sure where Kara and Tyson had gone, but he was. He should've known she wouldn't be able to sit and do nothing for long. He needed to get to her before his father did. Who knew how he'd react if he saw her on his territory.

Abe arrived with a plate of sandwiches. He set them down and reached into his pocket and took out a pill bottle. "You need to keep up your strength."

"We don't have time for all of this. I think Kara is on her way, if she's not already trying to break the door down.

"That's not good." He set the pills down next to the plate. "You eat and take your meds. I'll go keep an eye on the main entrance. If your father decides to check up on you, it would be best if he finds you here."

Noah growled in response, and his grandfather left. Tired, frustrated, and angry, he tossed the pills to the back of his throat and chased them down with half of a tuna sandwich. He wasn't hungry in the least, but while his mind spun trying to come up with a plan of action, he devoured half of the sandwiches.

Please let him get to Kara in time.

His eyelids grew heavy and his ears buzzed.

What the hell? Noah tried to read the label on the pill bottle, but all was a blur. His hand fell limply to his side, and the bottle fell from his grasp, scattering the pills all over the floor.

A shadow filled the doorway. *Gramps?*

Kara picked up a deck chair from the porch and held it up over her head. She was just about to smash the front window when the door swung open and Abe stepped outside.

"Noah was right." He shook his head at Kara. "You do realize if you smashed that window, the alarm system would alert everyone for miles, including Zachary."

She dropped the chair and ran to his open arms. "Oh, Abe, do you really think Joni is here?" She glanced behind him. "Where's Noah?"

Tyson stepped out of his truck and walked toward them.

"Why don't you park alongside the garage over there out of sight?"

Tyson put two fingers to his forehead and jogged back to the truck.

"We don't want Zachary to know you two are here if we can help it."

"I just don't understand why he'd do this. Where could he be?" Kara searched Abe's eyes.

"We saw his constant companion, Jeffery, leaving the west wing where Noah and his mother live."

"Oh, my God. Do you think he has her too?"

Abe shrugged. "I don't know anything for sure."

Tyson jogged up the pathway to the house and stood next to Kara. He stuffed his hands into his pockets and kept his head down.

"Follow me. I'll take you both to Noah," he whispered as he stepped inside the house. "There doesn't seem to be any staff on duty today, but keep it down just the same."

Noah's grandfather led them through a maze of impressive hallways before he finally ducked into one of the rooms.

Abe stood in the center of the room, scratching his head. "What the hell is going on?"

Kara noted an empty wheelchair and the contents of a pill-bottle strewn across the carpet. Her heart raced. "He has Noah now too, doesn't he?"

"All I know, is that I left Noah here while I went to find you." Abe coughed into his hand in a futile attempt to mask his upset.

"I'd like to know what the hell he hopes to accomplish by all of this." Kara threw up her hands, and flopped onto a chair.

Tyson put a hand on her shoulder. "Shouldn't we be doing something to find them?"

"How well do you know your way around the estate, Abe?" Kara gathered her faculties and sat at the edge of her chair.

"Well enough to get around." He picked up a napkin from the table to wipe his eyes, and blow his nose.

"If we go outside, would you know the way to Noah's wing of the estate? Maybe we can take a look in the windows."

Abe chewed the side of his mouth. "I think so."

"Well that's a start." She jumped to her feet. "I think there's less of a chance being detected this way."

Abe checked to make sure the coast was clear before taking them back out the way they'd come in.

"Which way now?" asked Kara once the three of them made it safely to the immaculate front lawn.

Abe leveled a hand above his eyes and pointed to his left. "Just up that way a bit is a courtyard. I think if we cut through there it will take us to where we want to be."

She took Abe's lead and stayed close to the building, ducking under the tall windows as they passed them. Kara's heart thumped madly in her chest. It seemed an awfully long time before they reached the courtyard began.

Abe leaned against the stone wall, his breathing labored.

"Are you okay?" Concerned, she squeezed his hand. He'd never looked so old and frail to her.

"I just need a minute to catch my breath." He wiped his wrinkled forehead with a crumpled hanky. "Phew! I'm too old for all of this." He feigned a smile.

"It's not too much farther is it?" Her patience grew thin. *I need to find Joni and Noah....now.*

Abe nod toward the far end of the deserted courtyard. "We'll turn right on the other side. That's where Noah's section of the Estate begins."

"I'm going to run ahead." Tyson broke his silence, and waited for Kara's consent.

"Go on, but keep down out of sight." Kara leaned over and kissed his warm cheek. "Be careful."

Tyson quickly looked away, but not fast enough to hide the

blush. His mounting concern for Joni further endeared him to her. She watched him slide along the stone wall effortlessly, not even breaking a sweat. *Oh to be young again.*

"You go with him, Kara. I'm slowing you both down." He suggested with heart-wrenching dejection in his tone.

Kara shook her head. "And have you go missing as well?" She squeezed his hand. "Are you ready to move on? How about you take the lead?" *...and set the pace you're comfortable with.*

Abe briefly closed his eyes. "You're quite a gal, Kara Walker.

Kara followed close behind him, down the length of the courtyard. A shrill whistle stopped them in their tracks. Up ahead, Tyson stood at the end of the courtyard waving animatedly.

"He's going to get us caught." Kara put a finger to her lips and gave him as stern a look as possible given the distance between them. Luckily, he seemed to catch the gist of what she tried to convey and squatted down to wait for them.

Kara reached him first, Abe at her heels. "What did you find? Do you see Joni?"

"I think I saw Noah's father. Follow me." He squat at the first window and put a hand out for them to stop. "Take a look," he whispered.

Cautiously, she crawled over to the window and peeked inside. Zachary Steele sat on a sofa, leafing through a magazine. Kara wanted to smash through the window and wrap her hands around his neck. She surveyed the room. A door opened, and the same butler from the previous night appeared and locked the door behind him. *Is that where he's keeping Joni and Noah?*

"His butler just locked that door behind him. Do you know where it leads to?"

Abe winced as he knelt to take a look. "That's Jeffery. If I remember correctly, that's the door to Glenda's room."

Tyson was already on his way to the next window. "I can't see in. I think the window is barred"

Kara joined him to find there were indeed bars on the other side of light fabric curtains. "Damn."

Abe tapped her shoulder. "I don't see any bars?"

“I think that’s what he wanted, to look like only curtains from the outside.”

He backed away from the window to sit on the grass. “I have an idea. Why don’t I pay my son a visit? I’ll act surprised to see him there and tell him I’m looking for Noah.”

“Oh no, I’m not taking any risks where you’re concerned.” *It’s bad enough the bastard has them. I’d never forgive myself if something happened to you.*

“Listen, Kara. I’m just going to distract him so you can maybe crack one of the panes enough to fit your hand through and move the curtain aside.” He looked intently into her eyes. “It’s the only way we’re going to find out if they’re in there.”

Kara hated the plan, but they didn’t have a lot of options. She had to admit it might just work. She sighed resignedly. “Okay, but you have to promise me if there’s any sign of trouble you’ll turn around and come back here with us.”

“I promise.” Abe kissed her cheek and winked. “Don’t you worry about me.” He turned to Tyson. “You take care of my girl.”

“Yes, Sir.”

Chapter Thirty-Two

"Something's wrong." Kara fidgeted with a tuft of grass she'd pulled out. "He should've made it there by now."

Tyson stretched out on his stomach. His eyes trained on the room. "He hasn't been gone that long, Kara. Let's give him a few more minutes."

Zachary Steele sat with Jeffery, seemingly engrossed in serious conversation. It took every ounce of her self-control not to smash the window and dive in at him. She readied herself for Abe's entrance, every nerve ending in her body on fire.

Tyson ripped a strip from the bottom of his t-shirt, and wrapped the fabric around a stone "Look." He nudged her arm and positioned himself in front of the window, stone in hand. "Hopefully the cloth will mute the noise of it hitting the glass."

A knock came to the door. The two men exchanged a curious look. Jeffery stood and walked over to the door and unlocked it.

Abe burst in and Tyson took his cue, tapping the glass hard enough to crack it. "Yes." He pulled out a sizeable shard.

Kara watched each face in turn. Not one of them flinched when the glass broke. She crawled to Tyson's side, and stuck her hand through the broken pane past the bars. Slowly, she moved the curtain aside. She gasped, and her free hand rose to her throat. Lying on a bed, covered in a plush comforter lay Noah, and beside him an older woman who she assumed was his mother. Next to the bed, stretched out on a chaise....*Joni.* All three appeared to be sleeping peacefully.

"Joni," She whispered as loud as she dared. Not one of them so much as flinched.

"Please let them be sleeping," Kara prayed. She sat back on her heels. "Now what in the hell are we supposed to do?" She wanted to shout for them to wake up, but knew it would alert Zachary.

I'd never make it there fast enough to stop him from hurting any one of them, or worse.

Tyson shrugged. "Abe is still arguing with his father."

Kara scooted over to see Zachary's face turn red, the veins on his neck bulging as he shook his finger at his son. "I'd give anything to hear what they're saying."

Zachary ended his tirade, and Abe calmly stared him down. He spoke a few words, shook his head in obvious disgust, and left the room. Zachary remained standing, his mouth agape, staring at the door. After a few seconds, he stormed over to a mini-bar behind a grand piano and poured amber liquid from a crystal decanter and tossed the drink back in one swallow. He refilled the glass and took it with him to sit back down on the couch. Jeffery opened his mouth to speak, and Zachary held up a hand, shaking his head.

Kara rolled back to the bedroom window to find not one of three had moved. The rise and fall of Noah's chest calmed her somewhat, but she knew, given the circumstances, there was no way the three of them were sleeping of their own accord.

An image of Caleb at Noah's bedside with a syringe in hand flashed in her mind. *If you have enough money, you can buy anything.*

Panic seized hold of her. *What if they've been drugged?* She crawled over to Tyson and grabbed the front of his shirt. "We have to get them out of there—*now.*"

His eyes grew big, and he covered her hands with his own. "Calm down, Kara. As soon as Abe gets back, we'll figure something out."

"I've got a bad feeling about all of this, Tyson. Do you think it's possible they've been drugged?"

Tyson searched her face, when all of a sudden he froze. The very real possibility hardened his expression. "We have to get them out of there."

Kara jumped to her feet between the two windows. "Let's head back the way we came. Maybe we'll see Abe on the way."

She ran faster than ever to keep up with Tyson's long strides.

They didn't bother ducking under the windows. The only people they feared seeing them, were back in those two rooms. The front door stood wide open, no sign of Abe anywhere. Inside, corridors branched out in three different directions.

"Which way do we go?" Kara gasped for air.

"West is this way."

They tore off down the hall, when suddenly Tyson came to an abrupt halt and held out his arms to stop her. Kara smacked into him, and he covered her mouth, muffling the string of curses on her tongue.

Tyson flattened his back against the wall and pulled her to stand beside him. He put a finger to his lips and nodded in the direction of the corner they were nearing. Confused, she strained to hear the voices. She took a deep breath and braved a peek around the corner.

"I don't care what it costs," Zachary spoke sternly to Jeffery.

"I could be awhile; you can't go to the drugstore and buy this stuff off of the shelf." He waved an empty vial in front of his boss's face.

"I know that. Where do you think the first batch came from? You have about an hour before the three of them start coming to." He jabbed a finger at his personal servant's bony chest. "You best be back before then."

Kara noted the flash of anger in Jeffery's eyes. "Yes, sir." He turned and hustled down the hall in the opposite direction.

Zachary stepped back into the room and closed the heavy wooden door behind him.

Kara sat with her back to the wall, trying to process what she'd just witnessed.

"If I heard right, Noah's father just sent Jeffery out to purchase heroine. Heroine intended for his wife, his own son, and my...Joni." She clenched her hands to fists. "We have less than an hour to come up with a plan."

"Maybe we should call the cops." Tyson rubbed his face.

"The last thing we want is a bunch of sirens spooking Zachary. God knows what he'd do if he felt he was cornered." Kara remembered the kind detective from the bakery incident. Maybe he'd be able to help.

"Listen, you stay here. Don't take your eyes off of that door. I'm going to find a phone."

"Are you going to call the cops?"

"I think we can trust the detective who handled things when Caleb totalled our kitchen." She feigned a smile. "If Abe shows up, keep him here, okay?"

"You be careful." He gave her a quick hug. "Please hurry!"

Kara fled down the hall, opening each door she came to and took a quick look inside. It wasn't until the sixth or seventh door she finally spotted a phone. She snuck into the room and sat behind the desk, and called information for the number to the precinct.

"Detective Spalding, please."

"One moment."

"Spalding here."

"Detective Spalding, this is Kara Walker, do you remember me?"

"Why yes I do. You're the lady from the bakery. How can I help you?"

Kara spelled out the situation as quickly as possible.

"Wait, are you telling me you're in the Steele Estate right now?"

"Yes, and I have someone watching the door to where Zachary Steele has the three of them drugged and locked in a bedroom."

"I want you to listen carefully. Under no circumstances are you to go in that room. Do you hear me?"

Silence permeated the phone line.

"Kara? I have officers enroute to the estate as we speak. We'll enter as quietly as possible so as not to alert Zachary. Promise me you won't try to handle Mr. Steele on your own?"

"I can't promise that. As long as Jeffery doesn't come back and Zachary stays put, I'll wait for you to get here."

Chapter Thirty-Three

Noah only managed to open his eyes a sliver. His body felt like it had been dipped in lead and left out to harden. He sensed he wasn't alone and summoned the strength to turn his head. He gasped, shocked to find his mother asleep beside him.

Across the room, a blurred image filled his limited line of vision. He blinked until the form took shape. *Joni?* A memory of Joni's disappearance surfaced in his mind. *Is Kara here somewhere? The pills, he'd taken his medicine....*

I was drugged? Now it made sense why he felt the way he did. Surely his own father didn't drug him? Did he drug Mother and Joni as well?

Noah contracted his muscles, to no avail. He didn't budge. If his mother woke up right now, how would she react to seeing two strangers in her room? Sadly, she hadn't remembered him as her son for a couple of years now.

He strained to hear, unable to tell if anyone was on the other side of the door. *I have to get up. What if whoever is responsible for this tries to drug us again? What if next time I don't wake up? Please God, let my mother and Joni wake up now.*

Noah clenched his teeth and managed to grip the side of the bed, despite his body fighting every move. Sweat beaded his forehead as he strained to pull himself up to sit. His head swam, the threat of darkness enveloping him again, very real. He concentrated on breathing....in and out, slowly until the threat passed.

A cool breeze whispered across his damp skin, directing his attention to the window, where the curtain billowed between bars....*Bars?* Who *put bars on the window?* Whoever did it, they made sure to put them in so only the curtain showed from outside Bars meant not to keep predators *out*....but captives *in*...

How did the pane get broken? Had someone discovered

them?

Kara?

A soft murmur interrupted the onslaught of questions jumbled in his mind. He watched Joni expectantly as her eyelids fluttered several times before opening wide. She looked all around the room before she found Noah.

He put a finger to his lips for her to keep quiet. Joni pressed her lips firmly together, and inch by inch, made her way to the end of the lounge and stood. She put one hand on the wall and the other to the side of her head, swaying slightly. She seemed so fragile, pale and terrified, so unlike the girl with the rosy cheeks and infectious smile who worked at the bakery.

"Come sit by me," whispered Noah. "I don't want to wake my mother if at all possible. I'm not sure how she'll react. She hasn't known who I am for some years now."

Compassion filled Joni's eyes...Kara's eyes. "I don't understand. What's going on?"

Noah held her hand. "I'm afraid it's my father. I'm pretty sure he drugged all three of us to bring us here."

Joni's eyes grew bright, brimming with unshed tears. "But why?"

Noah sighed. "He's a very bitter man and feels your mother is responsible for Caleb being in jail, amongst other things."

"That's ridiculous." She sat next to him at the side of the bed, careful not to disturb his mother.

Noah shrugged. "Maybe so, but he wants to make your mother suffer. I'm sure he thinks the best way to do so is through you."

"So what happens now?"

Noah shook his head. Behind him his mother groaned. His heartbeat quickened, and he held his breath. He glanced over his shoulder, relieved to see, she'd only turned in her sleep. "We have to find a way out of here. I don't know about you, but I can't just sit here and wait for something to happen."

Joni nodded vigorously. "Is that the only way out of here?"

"I'm afraid so, and Father has barred the window." The

curtain billowed slightly, reminding him of the broken pane. "If you stand on the chaise, do you think you will be able to see out the window?"

Joni didn't hesitate; she walked mindfully over to where she'd slept. She glanced at Noah's mother before she stepped up and stood on tiptoe barely able to see over the window ledge. "There's a broken pane," Joni *whispered.*

"Do you see anything else?" Just a piece of material, and...a rock."

Noah's mind raced. *Someone had deliberately broken the glass to see inside. Someone knows we're here. I pray it's my grandfather and not Kara. There's no telling what he'd do if he found her here.*

Joni stopped and pressed her ear against the door.

"Can you hear anything?"

She held up a finger, her brow creased. "There are at least two people talking out there."

"Do you recognize the voices?"

"Wait. Maybe it's just one person on the phone." She jerked back as if the door turned hot and pointed to show someone stood right on the other side. The doorknob turned from side to side before clear footsteps moved away.

Noah let out a breath he hadn't been aware of holding.

"Do you think he heard us?" Joni spoke just loud enough for him to make out what she asked.

Noah shrugged and curled his finger for her to come over to him. "We better be careful. Hopefully whoever is out there was simply checking to make sure the door was locked."

"I'm scared, Noah." Her voice cracked, and a single tear rolled down her pale face.

Noah lifted his arm and laid it over her shoulders, pulling her to his side. "You have to have faith, Joni. You know your mother isn't the type to sit idly by while you're missing. I bet she's trying to figure out a way to get to us as we speak."

Joni sniffed and laid her head on his chest.

Tyson sat with his back to the wall, keeping his eyes on the door to the west wing. He acknowledged Kara's return with a vacant smile.

"Any change?"

Tyson shook his head. "Did you find a phone?"

"Yes, help is on the way." Worry came over her. "I wonder what happened to Abe?"

"I don't know. I hope he's okay."

Her breath caught in her throat. The distinct click of the door opening filled the vacant hall. Zachary stepped out and looked from left to right. He glanced at his watch, and sighed in annoyance before stepping back into the room and closing the door.

"Jeffery must be taking longer than anticipated."

Down the hall, past the room, movement caught her attention. "Look." She pointed, unable to make out who it was.

Tyson jerked his head the other way and put a protective arm in front of Kara. From the opposite direction four men approached with weapons drawn, led by the detective.

Kara smiled and breathed a sigh of relief. "Thank God you're here."

"Which room is he in?" asked the Detective Spalding. He wore a baseball cap turned backwards, and held a hand gun.

"He's right in there. In a locked adjoining room; he has my daughter, his son, and his wife drugged."

The detective hand-signed to the officers at the opposite end of the hallway. "You stay right here."

Kara opened her mouth in protest but thought better of it. Any attempt to intervene might jeopardize her daughter's safety. She'd gladly leave this to the professionals.

The police hunkered down and swarmed the hallway. Without warning, they kicked in the door "Police! Put your hands in the air."

Kara darted out from around the corner and raced into the room to find the detective frisking a handcuffed Zachary Steele. "Do you have a key for that room?"

Zachary remained tight-lipped, lethal rage flashed in his eyes as he glared directly at her.

Kara lunged at him, pounding on his chest. "You sick bastard. Where's the key?"

Detective Spalding pulled her off of him. She stood panting, glaring at Noah's father. "Why? How could you do this to your own son and wife?"

"You've been nothing but trouble from the first day I heard your name mentioned. You've completely destroyed my family." Spittle flew in her direction as he verbally lashed out.

"Stand back." An officer kicked in the door. The sound of splintering wood filled the room. Kara bolted past him to find Noah and Joni huddled together on one the side of the bed. A wide-eyed woman sat up against the headboard, her knees drawn to her chest.

Kara threw herself at Noah and Joni, sobbing. "Thank God, you're okay."

Noah was first to pull away. "Let's get out of here. We're scaring my mother," he whispered to Kara.

Kara looked over his shoulder through a veil of tears, to see the terrified woman. There was no mistaking she was indeed his mother. An officer reached for Glenda's hand and she shrugged him away. Her gaze darted erratically around the room before settling on Noah.

She saw the pain in Noah's face as he tried to stand, and put a hand on his knee to stop him. "You wait here a minute. Don't try to stand, okay?"

His shoulders slumped and he bowed his head. Kara took Joni's hand and guided her from the room. Detective Spalding walked toward them.

"We need a wheelchair for Noah. There's one in the room where we discovered him missing."

The detective waved an officer over. "We need a wheelchair. Ms. Walker will tell you where to find one."

"That won't be necessary." Noah stood in the doorway.

Do NOT pass Go
Go Directly to JAIL

Chapter Thirty-Four

Half an hour passed since Detective Spalding left Kara alone in his office to question Joni and Tyson separately. She sat on her hands to stop from tidying the clutter on his desk. Newspapers, files, empty coffee cups, and the remnants of what looked like yesterday's lunch littered the desk's surface. Even his filing cabinet stood in disarray with files randomly sticking out here and there.

With all the commotion at the estate, she'd only gotten a fleeting glimpse of Noah as he was being whisked away to the hospital for observation, and as far as she knew, Abe still hadn't made an appearance. She clung to the hope, no news was good news.

Kara was on her feet the second she heard the click of the door handle. The detective entered his office. "I'm sorry to have kept you waiting so long, Kara." He pushed aside a stack of papers and sat on the corner of his desk.

"Where is my daughter?"

"She's fine. We're done with the questions for the time being. Both Joni and Tyson are waiting for you in the reception area."

"We're free to go?"

He nodded. "I've advised Joni to go get checked out by a doctor. We still don't know what drug he used to knock them out."

"I'll make sure she does. Has Noah's mother been examined?"

"Yes, her own doctor has gone out to the estate to be with her."

"Thanks for everything." Kara shook his hand.

"I'm just glad we were able to get there in time."

Kara feigned a smile. "You and me both."

Joni waved from the reception area where she sat, arm-in-arm, with Tyson.

"Before I leave, did you happen to find Abe Steele?"

Detective Spalding nod toward a closed office door. "We should be finished with him any minute."

"You mean he's here?" Relief washed over her.

"I guess you couldn't have known."

"Known what?" asked Kara.

"Your friend might very well have saved all of your lives."

She cocked a brow. "How so?"

"He must have spotted Jeffery upon his return to the estate. He took his SUV and pinned him against the wall, blocking him from being able to get out of his car."

"No kidding?"

"Jeffery had five full vials of an unknown substance in his possession. We're convinced they were intended for not only the three he'd abducted, but one for you, Kara and Abe."

Her jaw dropped at the same time as the office door opened, and a very tired looking Abe walked out. Kara flung herself into his arms, almost knocking him down.

"Easy now!" He laughed.

"I'm so glad you're okay. We were worried sick when you didn't come back."

Joni joined them, and the three embraced while Tyson stood back, shifting from foot to foot.

"Get over here," Kara ordered, her voice thick with emotion.

Tyson smiled sweetly and joined in the group hug.

Detective Spalding smiled broadly. "You're all free to go."

Kara broke away and wiped her eyes with the back of her hand.

"Where to now?" asked Joni.

"The hospital to get you checked out, and hopefully Noah will still be there."

Joni scrunched up her face. "I'm fine, Mom."

"We'll just make sure of that, won't we?"

"Yes, we will," Tyson chimed in.

Joni raised her hands in defeat. "No fair—two against one."

"Thank you." Noah smiled at the nurse. "This is the best I've felt since coming out of the coma."

"You should be having a massage daily. It will help improve the mobility of your joints and reduce the tension within your muscles." She wiped her oily hands on a towel.

"And it feels pretty good too." Noah raised his arm over his head with little effort. "Well I couldn't do that before now."

"Hello, Noah." Dr. Stouffer walked into the room with clipboard in hand. He peered over the rim of his glasses and smiled. "How are you feeling?"

"I think I might just make it after all." He quipped.

"Everything seems to check out okay. How do you feel about going home?" He closed the file and tucked it under his arm.

"You mean, other than the fact I'm not sure where home is?" Noah threw his hands up.

"Your home is with me." Kara stood in the doorway, clearly choked with emotion.

"Kara." Noah opened his arms and she ran into his embrace. He nuzzled her hair, breathing in the intoxicating scent of spring flowers and cinnamon. "I'm so sorry."

Kara pulled back. "What do you have to be sorry for?"

"My father...."

She put a finger to his lips. "You had no control over what your father did." She pushed the hair back from his face. "It's all over now."

Abe sniffled louder than warranted. "Sorry to interrupt, but Joni needs you to sign a paper."

Kara kissed Noah's forehead. "I won't be long."

He followed the sway of her slender hips as she left the room.

Abe shook his head. "You've got it bad." He clicked his tongue.

"Has there been any word about my mother?"

"She's a little shaken up and confused, but the doctor gave her something to help her sleep and Brenda is spending the night with her at the estate."

"That's a relief." He stared fixedly at his grandfather. "What about my father?"

Undeniable sadness filled his eyes. "I talked to my old friend, Judge Cookson. He expedited an order for a psychiatric assessment."

"That doesn't surprise me." Noah stood. "I've made a decision. I'm taking Mother far away from the Steele Estate."

"Not too far, I hope." Abe offered Noah his arm.

"I don't know where for sure." Noah leaned on his arm. He was still weak, but no longer felt like his limbs were coated in lead. "I need to talk to Kara."

"You need to talk to me about what?" Kara and Joni entered the room, followed closely by Tyson.

"I say we all get out of here." Abe put an arm around Kara and Joni.

"I'll second that motion. Let's all go back to my place. I'll put a pot of coffee on and we can all put our feet up."

Ada dissolved into tears upon seeing Kara and Joni and smothered them both with hugs and kisses. The day had taken a toll on Noah and he leaned heavily on Tyson to get down from the SUV.

Kara broke free from Ada and steered Tyson and Noah to the sofa in her living room. Once seated, she tucked a blanket around his legs and propped his feet up on a stool.

"Thank you, Kara."

His smiled stirred something deep down in her belly. "I'll put get the coffee perking, and put the kettle on for tea."

Ada followed her into the kitchen where she already had the kettle on to boil and had set out sandwiches and a platter of desserts from the bakery.

"I see you've thought of everything, as always." Kara clasped her hands.

"I came over as soon as Tyson called his brother. I thought you all might need a bite to eat." Ada leaned against the counter. "Are you okay?"

Kara sighed wearily. "I am now, Ada. It's been one hell of a day. I'll tell you all about it later. For now, I want to enjoy having everyone here, safe and sound. If Zachary Steele had succeeded in his plan, not one of us would be here to talk about it."

Ada fanned herself. "Oh my, what a brute that man is. I hope they lock him up and throw away the key."

A whistle filled the room. Kara made a move to tend to it, but Ada quickly shooed her away. "You let me take care of this. Go on and sit down. Noah hasn't taken his eyes off you since you got home."

She sneaked a look out of the corner of her eye. Noah sat holding Adam Love's romance novel in his hands. He lifted his head and smirked her way. She smiled knowingly and crossed the distance between them. She sat next to him on the sofa and took the book from his hands.

"I heard he's a best seller. Ever heard of him?" Kara teased.

"If I have, would it be a problem?"

She put the book down on the coffee table and melded to his side like it was the most natural thing to do. Now wasn't the time to discuss his writing. Noah shifted the blanket to cover her legs as well and held her hand. She laid her head against his arm and smiled at the roomful of people she cared most about.

Joni and Tyson sat together in an oversized armchair. She saw the gentle way he touched her and knew they were very much in love. Tyler helped Ada serve the tea and pass around the sandwiches. Abe grinned like a little boy upon seeing the tray of desserts.

Noah exchanged a knowing look with her.

"I think he's my biggest fan." Kara smiled warmly.

"Maybe your second biggest fan." He gazed intently into her eyes.

Kara's eyes filled with emotion as looked around the room. She squeezed Noah's hand. "This is the first time my house has felt like a home."

"Being laid up in a hospital bed gave me lots of time to think. What do you think about finding a house big enough for all of us?"

Kara's heartbeat quickened. "What do you mean all of us?" Did she dare assume he was asking her to do something she swore she'd never do again?"

"I mean you and Joni, Ada and my mother, and my grandfather if he'll consider it."

Kara's watched Abe pat Ada's hand. They smiled at one another before continuing their conversation.

"I don't think it would take much convincing." She winked playfully. "What about your mother?"

"I've been thinking...what if she had a suite of her own? Do you think Ada would agree to a roommate? She really isn't any bother, and a nurse would come in every day to make sure she takes her medication. I'm sure Brenda will insist on keeping her job as housekeeper. My mother and she have become very close."

"I think that's a wonderful idea. Ada won't be quite as lonely if she has your mother for company."

What does this mean for us?

Noah tossed back the blanket and inched his way to the edge of the sofa.

Kara offered her hand to help but he pushed it away.

"Please. I need to do this on my own." Awkwardly, he slid himself off the couch and fell to his knees.

Kara tried to help, but instead he took her hand in his and looked deeply into her eyes.

Confused, her eyes slowly widened as she realized his intention.

A hush fell upon the room.

"I know we haven't really had much time together, but I feel like I've known you all my life."

Her hand flew to her mouth, and she stifled a sob.

"One thing I've learned through this whole ordeal is we have no guarantees there will be a tomorrow." He pressed his lips to her fingers. "I can't take a chance on losing you." He swallowed hard. "Kara Walker, will you make me the happiest man alive and marry me?"

In that instant, all reservations fell to the wayside. The love she saw in his eyes warmed her to the core. She glanced over at Joni. Tears spilled down her daughter's rosy cheeks, and she smiled her approval.

Moisture filled Kara's eyes and she cupped the side of his face. "Yes, Noah. I would be honoured to be your wife."

He covered her lips with his, and the room erupted in clapping and tears. She'd finally have the happy family she always dreamed of. They may not all be related by blood, but they shared something even more binding—a deep and unbridled love for each other that started by choice and would last a lifetime.

The End

ABOUT THE AUTHOR

Adelle Laudan lives in Southern Ontario with an 8-lb diva dog named Chachi, who always manages to make her laugh. She is Mom to four and Gramma to Lexxi and Logan. Her daddy was a preacher and often joked, ˜If he's not wearing Harley Davidson underwear, she ain't interested'.

Adelle invites you to travel the many twists and turns her stories will take you. Be sure to fasten your seatbelt, it promises to be a ride you won't soon forget.

http://adellelaudan.com

Adelle's Books
Heart of Steele
Dear Angel
Iron Horse Rider Trilogy
In Your Eyes
Killer Scents / Scent of a Killer

Short Stories
Crucified
Serenity

Free Reads
Solidarity
Timeless Encounter

Women of Strength Series
Juliana
Rosa
Shani
Kat
Grace
Dani
Eva

Adult Reads
She Rides
Mystified
Tattoo Rain –Feb 14th, 2014

www.ingramcontent.com/pod-product-compliance
Lightning Source LLC
Chambersburg PA
CBHW051957220626
47052CB00004B/974
9781927700037